Frank's Sky High Wishes

by
Helen MacEachern

Best wishes

Helen Mac Eachern

Cover Art by Jesse Lemire

Published by:
A Snowy Day Distribution & Publishing
P.O. Box 2014
Merrimack, NH 03054
(603) 493-2276
www.ASnowyDay.com

Editor: Cynthia N. Godin

First Edition

ISBN: 978-1-936615-18-6

Printed in the United States of America

Sincere thanks to Sherie, Tammy, and most of all, my daughter, Linda, for all their encouragement in bringing this book to completion.

I'm Frank Brendan. I'm thirty-six years old, and I've never been married. Two days ago, I received this letter from my teenage girlfriend of long ago.

Frank Brendan
220 E. Whitewash Road
P.O. Box 324
Middle, Oklahoma 24382

March 20, 2009

Dear Frank,

I still remember to this day the moment you told me you were leaving Providence to go with your parents, brothers, and sisters to take over your grandparents' farm in Oklahoma. It was quite a shock to me as I was so sure that you and I were deeply in love and would eventually be married. However, I understood how you felt about going with your family. It was something you had to do. There were no choices in the matter.

We did keep in touch - at first - but it wasn't till you were gone for two months and I graduated from high school that I realized I was pregnant with your child. I had started dating Hal

1

Farmer, an Army man, such a wonderful man that I just had to be up front and honest about the baby I was carrying. He loved me, he told me, and well, I loved him back. So when I was five months along, Hal and I married.

We and our little girl, Sky, traveled a lot. To my - and Hal's - disappointment, we had no other children; and so we poured all our devotion onto our wonderful little girl.

Two years ago, Hal was killed in action. Sky and I were devastated. I thought we would never get over losing him. Now, my poor little Sky has more sorrow coming her way. You see, I have cancer. Doctors say I don't have long to live.

Sky has no one but me. My parents, as you know, are missionaries and are now in Africa. There is no way she can go to live with them - and I don't want her to. I am so terrified that if she did go there, she would just languish in her grief - suffer and die from it all.

Please, Frank, take Sky to live with you. I remember how wonderful your entire family was. Give her the love she needs, Frank. Let her become a member of your big family. I know the best place for her to be is with you.

My next door neighbor, Bernice Manning, has your name, address, and phone number. She will guide Sky in my last rites and closing up the house, etc.

I've told Sky that I'm dying and about my last wish for her to go to live with you, her biological father. She is thrown off balance by all this as I am sure you must be, but I feel deep down in my soul that neither one of you will ever regret this.

I am enclosing Sky's birth certificate and a current picture of her. Isn't she beautiful?

All my love,

Marie

CHAPTER ONE

June 1992, I was eighteen and living in Providence, Rhode Island with my parents and my three brothers and two sisters. One day - oh, it must've been around noontime - Mom got an upsetting call from Nanny. Mom held herself together fairly well, for Nanny's sake, but I could tell Mom was struggling with her mother's sobs surging through long-distance telephone lines.

Apparently, Poppy had given Nanny a very bad scare the day before. He had wandered off and had gotten all the way to the Snake River where he started to wade into the fast-moving flow. Thank goodness, two fishermen who knew Poppy well spotted him. Those two small town folks knew Poppy had never been the best of swimmers - even in his younger days - so they sauntered over to him and discovered he didn't have a clue as to where he was or where he was going. So they brought him home to Nanny. She hurried him off to Doctor Barry Stone who confirmed what she had been dreading for a couple of months: Poppy had Alzheimer's disease.

Doc Stone was sure Poppy had the slow-moving kind and so prescribed a medicine called Namenda, which would not stop the disease, but might slow it down even more. He told Nanny that Poppy's future was not good and that running the dairy farm was something that before long was going to be beyond him.

So it was that Nanny asked Mom to move our family to Middle, Oklahoma to live and run the dairy farm. My grandparent's house was so big it could accommodate our entire family.

Mom sank onto the chair beside the phone, stammering, "Y-yes, Ma. I-I know Middle is a terrific town to bring up family in..." She paused, listening. Then she said, "Uhm, no, Ma... Honest. You are not putting me on the spot. I..."

I could tell my mother was fibbing.

"I-I will speak to Tom...and the children. Yes... This evening... And if this is something we can do, I... Yes, Ma, I know it's best if we came right away... Ma, listen to me... I am sure Dad has lots of his good ol' intelligent days left and..."

Another fib.

When my mother finally hung up, she ran her palms up and down her hips. She turned and spotted me standing in the doorway. A weak smile wrinkled her lips - and mine.

You could have heard a pin drop after Mom relayed Nanny's request at the supper table. Moments slogged by.

Dad heaved a sigh. Prying himself up off his chair, he said, "Well, Jean, I'm all for this move. I've been expecting a lay-off any day."

I squinted at him. Layoff? I thought. Well, that was news to me.

"There have already been six men laid off," Dad continued, "and I figure I'm next to go."

Mom gasped. "Tom! How come you didn't say something?"

Dad gave her a sappy look, which he did every time he looked at her, then stepped over and placed his right hand on her shoulder. "You have enough worries on your plate, Jean. Keeping a family this size on the straight and narrow is no easy task - for any human being."

She smiled up at him then kissed the back of his hand.

My fourteen-year-old sister, Lisa, exchanged twinkles of the eyes with my ten-year-old sister, Susan. Their hands cupped their mouths, squelching giggles.

So the entire family was on board; well, except for me, I suppose. The thought of leaving Marie didn't set all that well in my belly. Plus there was my new job I had gotten after graduating high school. But then the memory of my visit to Nanny and Poppy's farm, two years ago, floated into my head - and then the wish I had had since then about someday living there.

Mom called Nanny that very night, despite knowing full well that Nanny and Poppy went to bed with the chickens. On the other hand, she knew Nanny was more than likely pacing the floor, worried sick, anxious to hear our decision. Nanny was quite relieved that we would soon be there.

Later that night, I sprawled across my bed in the room I bunked with my three brothers, sixteen-year-old John and Joey and ten-year-old Leo. We mulled over the photos I had taken during my summer on Nanny and Poppy's dairy farm. Even though I had gone off at the mouth about the place when I got home back then, now, my brothers were actually listening to me - and this time, I sold them.

CHAPTER TWO

We settled right into Nanny and Poppy's dairy farm and the town of Middle as though we had always lived there. We thought of ourselves as being the Walton's of the twenty-first century. Yes, we had a grandmother, a grandfather, even a "John-boy". John filled that spot pretty good as he was the only boy I knew of who kept a journal. He also got a job at the town newspaper, The Middle News. On the other hand, he became fascinated with crime paperback books, so he ended up quitting the paper and taking a job as a deputy at the Sheriff's Office.

Every one of us worked in the barn. Poppy was able to teach Dad and the rest of the family how to run the farm before the illness took over his brain. From then on, we had Howie, Poppy's barn foreman, a man who had the patience of Job. We learned how to hose down walls and ceilings and wash manure out of stalls. Our first thoughts were *Yuck!* But soon it got to be no big deal. In fact, we got to clowning around at times, and a cow pie or two were known to fly. Like I said, Howie had the patience of Job.

Nanny was a great cook. Between her and Mom, none of us even came near a hunger pang.

We all had the job of looking out for Poppy. We did everything we could think of to keep him safe; and that was the hardest job of all. It was good there were so many of us, since the man we all loved so dearly evolved into a peppy toddler who wandered off without a second thought. We were truly blessed to be living in a town where, if he slipped through our fingers, someone always brought him home.

It was so nice seeing Nanny hugging Poppy, patting his hand, reassuring him. "Poppy and I are so happy all of you are here in Middle with us."

Dad was the real surprise. Not one of us thought of him as a man who might become a farmer of any sort. Amazing how he thrived. He was constantly working to keep the farm and the dairy and the house shipshape. And he took on Mom's parents as his own.

As for me, I was in my glory. Ever since that summer I had spent on my grandparents' dairy farm, my destiny was sewn up.

Four years later, Poppy died in his sleep. Gosh, we missed him so.

Joey went off to veterinary college. Susan earned a Masters Degree in Teaching at State College. Lisa, after attending a high-mucky-muck university in Illinois, became a lawyer. She was the only sibling who did not return to Middle. Still, she only lived a few miles away in Oakridge, so nobody complained - much. Lisa never got married. Neither did I. Bottom line is: Leo and I were the only siblings who ended up farmers.

When Leo graduated high school, he wanted to settle down. He wanted to marry his girlfriend, Heather, who was a year older than him. They dreamed of having their own farm, planting all kinds of vegetables, the whole ball of wax; so as a wedding gift, Mom and Dad and Nanny gave Leo and Heather a sizable piece of land, which had been part of the original dairy farm. I gave Leo and Heather five laying hens and with the help of John and Joey, built the finest henhouse you'll ever see in this lifetime - a henhouse a heck of a lot better than that mobile home Leo and Heather were living in.

Eventually, Leo and Heather broke ground for their house, which took quite some time, since they wanted to build it themselves and needed outside income to fund it. Heather held down a full-time job, working in Doc Stone's office while Leo worked at the local feed and grain store, a job that was supposed to be part time, but routinely went beyond forty hours a week.

Shortly after Poppy died, Nanny went down to Texas to live in a senior citizen mobile home park. Some good friends of hers lived in Texas, so she was quite content. After a couple of years, we found out she was ill, so Mom and Dad decided to sign over the farm to me and retire, moving to Texas to be near to Nanny, so they could care for her. By that time, the farm was supporting me, three full-time workers, four part-time workers, and Dolly, the live-in housekeeper. While I was a bit nervous about taking on such responsibility, Mom and Dad insisted, "You will handle the farm just fine."

CHAPTER 3

One April day in 1999, I was walking from the barn to the house when I heard the kitchen phone ring. I stepped it up and tore open the screen door. Snagging the phone in one hand, I yanked open the refrigerator door with the other. "Hello," I said while grabbing an apple.

"For crying out loud," Joey said, "when are you going to remember to take your cell phone with you?"

"Sorry about that," I said then bit a good size chunk out of the apple. As I crunched I could not help but think how I'm the oldest in my family of six and I should be more responsible. I swallowed half the mouthful then said, "What's up?"

"That little fella you wanted needs picking up," Joey said. "Today?"

My mind went blank. "Fella?"

"That litter of golden retrievers?" Joey prodded. "The one I'm saving for you?"

"Oh, yeah," I said. "Yeah."

Joey snorted. "The dawn cometh."

I ignored his snide remark. "I'll be by in a while. Howie is in the barn taking care of things, so I am free. Just let me get cleaned up, okay? I'll be along."

I was about to hang up when I heard "Oh wait."

I pressed the phone against my ear. "What?"

"Stop by Louie's, will ya?" Joey said. "Get me a chicken salad sub."

"Sure," I said. Well, I thought, I'm not just picking up a pup, I'm also free delivery.

By the time I got to Louie's Pizza and Sub Shop, it was crowding 11:30. As I got out of my truck, I spotted a boy, all alone, sitting on the bus stop bench outside Louie's - at least, I thought the kid was a boy. I did a double take. Yup, a boy. But he was so fair-skinned; plus that long blonde curly hair of his gave pause to question gender. Talk about being in need of a serious trim. There were no signs of ears at all.

His large, dark blue eyes slid me a sad look.

Gosh, he's thin as a rail, I thought. I scanned the area. Strange him being all alone like that. Maybe his mother or father was in one of these stores? Humph. I went into Louie's and ordered Joey's chicken sub and a pastrami on rye for me. While waiting, I spied on the boy.

Louie spoke up, "That kid ain't moved a muscle since planking down on that bench."

"How long has he been there?" I asked.

"An hour or so."

"Who is he?"

"No clue." Louis handed me the sandwiches.

I forked over cash and then headed out.

Those large, dark blue eyes slid me another sad look.

I smiled and gave a little wave as I passed him. Something ate at me. Something wasn't right here.

Joey's Vet Clinic was very impressive. Well, it really wasn't Joey's. It belonged to his boss, Doctor Harrigan, who was on an extended vacation - as usual. Must be nice. Anyways, Joey and I ate in the back room. Between bites, I told him about the boy on the bench. "I got a bad feeling about that whole situation."

Joey sloughed it off. "His parents picked him up by now. Come on. Let's take a gander at that litter of retrievers."

Talk about feisty pups! They were jumping all over each other, tripping over each other, you name it. I squatted down to watch and ended up sitting on the floor, Indian-style. I could have spent the entire afternoon doing that.

One pup, the bravest of the bunch, instigated numerous spats. "Boy!" I exclaimed. "That pup certainly is a handful!" I reached for him, but his silky little body was all muscle with not one single handle for me to hold on to. As he wriggled free of my grasp, my confidence waned.

"Geez, Joey, I don't know anything about raising a dog."

"You'll be great at it," Joey said, disappearing into another room.

I got to my feet. Dusting myself off, I appraised the situation - over-analyzing as I was known to do.

Joey came back bearing a book. He handed it to me. "All you need to know is in this."

"All I need to know?" I echoed, squinting at the cover.

"About dogs, big brother. About dogs."

Joey snagged the feisty pup and jammed him against my chest. "I got a cage you can borrow, but confine him only when need be."

"Like when he's in my truck?" I asked. "What if he does a job on my truck?"

Joey chuckled. "Listen, Frank. You, yourself, have managed to do an awful job on that ol' hunk of junk over the years, so don't go blaming an innocent puppy."

Maneuvering the pup into the cage was quite a task. Needless to say, he was quite unhappy in there.

On the way home, I stopped off for dog stuff at Abby's This & That Store, which is next door to Louie's. I felt bad about leaving the pup inside that dreadful cage, crying and crying like the baby he was. But I just couldn't take him out of that cage. How would I ever get him back into it?

It was almost 2:00 by then and the boy was still sitting on that bench. What a sad little fellow. Were those worry-lines on his face? "You need help with anything?" I asked.

"Nah." He stumbled over his words as though he didn't believe them himself. "Mom is coming to get me. Any time now."

I felt like doing something, but what? I swallowed hard then went into the store. I was the only customer, so I had Abby's complete attention. While picking out a collar and a leash, I mentioned the boy.

"Poor little guy," she said. "He's been there such a long time."

"Where the heck are his parents?" I asked.

Abby shrugged. "Bed and food."

"Huh?"

"You need a bed for that pup of yours - and food."

With a jerk of my chin, I said, "Ah!"

While Abby was bagging dog goodies, I peered out the window. The boy was focused on something up the street: a car; a man got out of it. While the man reached into the backseat, the boy jumped to his feet and ran down the alleyway between Abby's This and That Store and Louie's Pizza and Sub Shop. I couldn't help but picture the boy hunkered down behind trash containers.

The man headed over to the bench. He stood there, glaring up the street, glaring down the street. I tried to read the look on his face. Confusion? Anger? Apprehension?

"What's going on?" Abby asked, stepping up behind me.

I told her what had happened, and for about fifteen minutes, we scrutinized the man. His lips clenched. Then he stomped back to his car and took off with shrieks of bald tires.

Abby and I gawked at one another and then rushed to the back door. Outside, we discovered the boy hiding, flat beneath torn-up cardboard boxes. I offered him my hand. "That man is long gone."

Relief blanketed the boy's features.

Again I offered my hand.

This time the boy took it and got to his feet.

"Why did you run away from him?" Abby asked. "Your mother may have sent him to get you, you know."

"No!" Agitation laced with fright and wracked the boy. "Mom didn't send him! She would never send him for me!"

"Who is he?" I asked.

"Jake Burke! I'll never live with him again! You can't make me!"

I took the boy gently by the shoulders. "Nobody's going to make you do anything. Now, who are you anyways?"

"Brad."

"Last name?"

He eyed me.

I didn't push the issue. Sooner or later, the name would surface. "So what's up with this Jake fella?"

"He lived with Mama and me a while back. I hate him! He belted me around! And he hit Mama, too."

Abby spoke up, "Better run all this by the sheriff, Frank."

I ran my hand through my hair. "Yeah." I scrutinized the boy. "Okay, Brad, you stay here with Abby while I go to speak the sheriff."

Brad looked scared.

Abby rubbed her hand over Brad's upper arm. "The sheriff is Frank's brother. His name is John. He's a good man and won't do a thing to put you in any danger."

I started for the door then stopped. "On second thought, I could use some help, myself. Listen, Brad, I got my new pup in the truck and…"

"The puppy's been out there in that broken down old truck all this time?" Abby shrieked.

I gave her a sheepish look. "Well, yeah…"

"You never had a puppy before, have you?"

I waved my head side to side.

"Well, buster, you have a few surprises coming. Puppies have a great way of doing a lot of pooping."

"Guess I need to put a diaper on him."

Abby roared with laughter. Brad held back, yet a squeak or two leaked out.

"Anyhow, he's in a cage," I said, gathering up my purchases.

Abby winced. "Oh, my. That poor little fellow is probably wallowing in his own mess."

"Help me carry all this dog stuff out to the truck, will you, Brad?"

When we got to the truck, the pup was whining and wiggling, and the odor was atrocious. I got the collar and leash out of the bag and handed them to Brad. I took the pup out of the cage and handed him to Brad. I put the collar on the pup and snapped on the leash. "Take him for a walk, Brad, while I load the cage into the bed of the truck. That cage is going to need a good washing down."

Abby hollered out the door, "Bring him to the back door, Brad. I'll get some dry shampoo and towels and we'll clean him up."

I headed across the street to the Sheriff's Office. Upon entering, I recognized Charles Woodwood, owner of a pig farm five miles out of Middle. I did a little pacing while he and John finished their discussion. When Charles left, John turned to me. "What brings you here today, Frank?"

I took a seat across the desk from him and told him about what had gone down with Brad.

"What can I do? I can't leave him. He's scared. I have to take him home with me. I have to help him."

John made a clicking sound out one side of his mouth. "Not many choices here, that's for sure." He leaned back in his chair and scratched his chin. "It comes in handy to have a lawyer in the family. I'll give Lisa a call and ask her what we can do legally to take the boy under our wing. I'll get back to you, Frank, or I'll have her call you directly."

I went back across the street and told Abby I was taking Brad to my place. "If anyone comes around looking for him, don't tell them anything. On second thought, tell them to talk to the Sheriff." I turned to Brad. "John says it's okay for me to take you to my place."

"But what if Mom shows up?" Brad asked.

"I'll keep an eye out for her," Abby said.

Brad sat in the passenger seat, holding the pup, and was very pleased with the task. I glanced over at them and smiled. "The pup needs a name."

"I already got one."

"Yeah? Mind telling me?"

"Buddy."

I pursed my lips, giving it consideration. I nodded. "Buddy it is."

CHAPTER FOUR

Upon driving into the farm, I noticed Brad looking quite impressed. "So," I said. "Where do you live?"

"All over the place. Mama says we don't have much money, so it's cheaper to move than pay rent."

"Does she work?"

"Sometimes. Usually bosses aren't good to her, so she quits."

"Where were you born?"

He shrugged.

"You don't know where you were born?"

He eyed me. "Don't be be silly. I was a baby. How was I supposed to remember that?"

I pulled the car up to the back door. "What about your father?"

He shrugged.

I switched off the key. "Boyfriends?"

He rolled his eyes.

"Nobody ever helped with food or rent?"

"No!" he cried, reaching for the door handle. "Of course not! Men don't do that!"

I sat there for a moment, staring at the empty passenger seat. This was some fine mess, I thought. I took a deep breath. "Okay!" I got out of the truck. "What do you say, Brad? Let's get Buddy and his gear into the house."

Dolly, my housekeeper, was in the kitchen, cleaning up. She picked up her apron and wiped her hands on it while turning to us.

"This is Brad," I said. "He'll be staying with us a day or so." I figured I would explain his dilemma to her when he was out of hearing range.

"Nice to meet you, Brad," she said. She spied the puppy in his arms. "And who is this little sweetie?" She stepped over and caressed the pup's ear.

"Buddy," Brad said, just above a whisper.

"I'm hoping Brad might put in some time while staying here to get Buddy's training started," I said.

"Oh, what a little angel," Dolly cooed.

"I have to say, Dolly, you are taking this rather well," I said. "This means a lot more work for you."

"Stop it, Frank. Now, have you two eaten?"

"I did," I said. "Brad hasn't eaten today."

"You poor child!" she belched, "You must be starved!" She shook her finger at me. "Shame on you, Frank. Why didn't you feed him?"

"B-b-but...I..." I stammered. I was about to say I had guessed about him not eating.

The spread Dolly laid out on the table could have fed the entire United States Army. I had no idea the refrigerator could hold that much food. "When Brad is done eating," she said, "I'll show him around the house and bunk him in the spare bedroom."

I found out later that he thought he had died and gone to heaven by coming here. He had never had a bedroom of his own.

"Talk about beat," Dolly said, returning to the kitchen. "He no sooner laid down on the bed to test it out when he dropped off to sleep. He's snoring up a storm."

"Guess we won't be seeing him for a quite a while," I said.

"Go get his suitcase and I'll..."

"Suitcase?" I echoed.

"Don't tell me he doesn't have any clothes."

I smacked my forehead. "Boy, am I a dunce."

Her look seemed to agree. "Well, my grandson, Jason, is Brad's size. I'll borrow some of his clothes until we get Brad sorted out."

"Speaking of sorting out," I said. I told her about the day's events and then the phone call I was expecting from either John or Lisa. Dolly promised to holler for me if the call came while I was out at the barn. She gently reminded me, "You do have a cell phone, you know."

I twisted up one side of my face then headed out to the truck. I drove to the barn then unloaded the cage and hosed it down. "Boy, that pup must've pooped his brains out."

I hauled the cage into the milking barn. Howie and the other workers were bringing the cows in to be milked. While helping to hitch suction cups to teats, I repeated the day's events. Howie laughed at the thought of me dealing with a pup. "I hope you have a lot of newspapers to lay out and catch all that manure. And count on him keeping you up all night with his yelping."

My cell phone rang. I wormed my hand into my pocket then fished it out. I flipped it open and stuck it to my ear. "Yeah?"

"Call Lisa," Dolly said and then hung up without so much as a goodbye.

So I called Lisa on my cell phone. "Have you any words of wisdom for me?" I asked, hopefully.

"Only that you really must take care of that kid. Sending him back to the scene he's been in is something you just can't do. I spoke to a child services advocate by the name of Maryanne Reardon. She says Brad needs to be protected; however, that protection must be done legally. She says she'll be over to see you and Brad tomorrow and check out you and your home. She's bringing paperwork for you two to fill out."

When I went back to the house, Brad was in the kitchen playing with Buddy. Looks like Buddy was not going to be my dog.

Dolly hurried into the kitchen; and while checking an apple pie in the oven, she said, "My daughter, Shelby, is bringing over clean clothes for you, Brad. You can take a shower and change into them while I put the clothes you're wearing through the washer."

"We'll spread newspapers on the washroom floor and put Buddy in there for the night," I said.

Shelby came in a short while later, loaded down with clothes. She and I became friends that summer I spent on my grandparents' farm. We always enjoyed catching up with each other, so we hunkered down at the table and jabbered on and on while Dolly took Brad upstairs to show him how to fine-tune the antiquated shower. Meanwhile, Buddy weaved in and out and around our ankles, stopping only to gnaw on the toes of our leather shoes.

Shelby's husband Carol Panouski was the only child of a Russian couple who immigrated to the States when he was two years old. He and Shelby fell in love when they were in their senior year of high school. He was a mechanic, a very good one. He could fix anything from cars to farm machinery to washing machines. The small town of Middle kept him very busy.

"Will Brad be going to school here?" Shelby asked.

"Maryanne Reardon will determine that tomorrow," I said. "I don't even know if he'll be allowed to stay here."

"I can't see any reason for him not to stay," Shelby said. "But anyway, my Jason is looking forward to showing Brad around school. There are so few boys his age. I'm sure the two will become pals just like you and I did. Brad will be in the swing of things in no time at all."

Suddenly, Buddy darted for the stairs. Brad was on his way down. At the bottom of the stairs, the boy bent and picked up the jubilant puppy. How wonderful to see the two cuddling. At that moment, I realized that getting Buddy at this time was a real blessing for both of them - oh, and for me, too.

At supper, I asked Brad, "Have you been going to school?"

"Now and then. I can read okay, but I'm real good at math."

"Math was my strong suit, too," I said. "But I have to admit, I had to grow into reading. Now, I check out books at the Library all the time."

"I did that a lot at the last place Mama and I lived."

"Where was that?"

"Holly, Oklahoma."

Dolly spoke up. "An address will help to get your school records and to place you in the right grade."

Brad searched his memory. "I think it was 212 Suncrest... I think it was Avenue not Street."

Dolly jotted the complete address on the chalkboard next to the door. Turning, she caught Brad offering food from his plate to Buddy. "Bad idea, Brad. You're encouraging the pup to beg at the table. Not only can it be annoying to guests, but also, his own food is better for him."

I winked at Brad then offered Buddy some food from my plate.

Dolly tisked.

Later on, she washed the dishes. I dried. "You should adopt Brad?" she said.

"It's crossed my mind."

"He's a good kid, Frank."

I nodded. "If I adopted him, would you mind taking on his care with me?"

She laughed. "Do I really need to answer that question?"

"Sorry."

"Look, Frank, this house has so much room, it seems proper to have children in it. Puppies. Cats, rats, and unicorns, too. I'd mother all of them. So make Brad your son, I say. That boy couldn't pick a better father."

"I sure would like to be a dad," I said. "I know my family will be happy - even though I'm not married. Though they'd rather I did get married and have a son the usual way."

I mulled over the prospects for an hour or two. I called Mom and Dad. The day's events amazed them. They were even more amazed about me considering adoption. Mom thought it was a great idea, but Dad warned, "You know, the boy might have a father who will give you a hard time. Make sure you have all the information you need before going forward."

"We just don't want you to get hurt, dear," Mom added.

"I'll do all I can not to let that happen," I said. "One way or the other, Brad has led a hard life. Dolly and I are anxious to give him a good one. Anyways, I got to go. I want to talk to John and Joey."

John was glad I called. "How's the kid doing?"

"He seems okay."

"It's good you took him in, Frank. With me being sheriff and all, you'd think I'd be more like Dad and see the bad side of what might come of taking in a boy we know nothing about."

"Lisa has been a big help," I said. "She's arranged for a child services advocate to come here tomorrow."

"That's great," John said. "Hey, something's coming in on the squawk box. Talk to you later."

I hung up and then dialed Joey's number. Upon hearing Brad and Buddy had become great pals, he laughed. "Time will tell if you've gained a son, but one thing for sure, you lost a dog."

After that, I called Leo and brought him up to speed. I didn't talk long. Guess I was all talked out. Although, he did ask me to bring Brad over for a visit. I promised I would then said goodbye.

Before going off to bed, Brad and I spread newspapers, inches thick, across the washroom floor. When Brad put Buddy in there and closed the door, Dolly said, "I hope the pup snuggles down in his bed and goes to sleep, but I don't expect the night will be all that peaceful in this house. Expect him to do a lot of whining. Well, I'm on my way home now."

That night, for two long, long hours, Buddy whined, I mean wailed. Then all was quiet. In the morning I peeked into the washroom and found out why. Brad had brought down a pillow and blanket and had camped out with the pup. There they were, all snuggled up, sleeping blissfully.

CHAPTER FIVE

Maryanne Reardon arrived about 11:15 the next morning. She was a plain, no nonsense, middle age lady. She and I sat down at the kitchen table. Brad remained outside, playing with Buddy. "Tell me, Frank, how did you come to have Brad in your home?"

I knew she already knew all that, but I went over it anyway. As I did, Dolly joined us and was quite helpful at outlining the life I wished to give Brad. She also pointed out the chalkboard and the address Brad had given us.

Many more questions followed. Maryanne Reardon wrote down each and every answer quite thoroughly. Finally, she took a long hard look at me. Then she said, "At this point, I must speak with Brad."

I cleared my throat then got up and stepped outside. Earlier, I had explained to Brad the reason Maryanne Reardon was coming. I had told him she was going to ask him questions that might seem silly to him or questions he might not like at all. Even so, I expected him to speak freely and above all, expected him to be truthful. Now, I feared his answers just might dash this single man's sky high wishes of having a family of my own.

Maryanne asked to be left alone with Brad. I figured she must think Dolly's or my presence might influence him or cause him to hold his tongue.

Dolly and I slunk out of the kitchen, but didn't go far. No, we hugged either side of the kitchen doorframe, our ears pealed.

"First thing, Brad, I need to know your last name."

"Lapinski."

"Were you happy living with your mother?"

"I guess so. That is, until she let Jake Burke in the house."

"Do you want to go back?"

"Not if Jake is there."

"Tell me about Jake Burke."

"He's mean. Very mean. He smacks Mama and me around a lot and tells me all the time I'm bad. He takes off his belt and whips my bum with it, over and over again."

"Does your Mama think you are bad?"

"No."

"Does she spank you?"

"Not really."

"What do you mean, 'Not really'?"

"Well, when Mama gets mad? Like when I spill my milk? She puts out cigarettes on me."

"Where?"

I leaned around the doorframe and watched Brad roll up his sleeve and extend his arm to her. My jaw dropped. So many cigarette burns! Why didn't I know? I hated myself. Why didn't I question him about wearing long sleeves? Especially after all the warm days we had? As tears rose in my eyes, I noticed Maryanne staring at me. I drew back, outside the doorframe. I heard her ask, "Would you like to live here, Brad, on the farm with Frank and Dolly?"

"I sure would."

"Frank? You and Dolly come back now."

As I pulled myself together, Dolly took a tissue out of her apron pocket and dabbed moisture off my face. She took me by the arms, gave me a reassuring look then turned me around and nudged me into the kitchen.

"We have lots of paperwork to sign," Maryanne said, taking forms out of her briefcase.

Brad trained his baby-blues on me. "Buddy is staying, too, right Frank?"

"Only if you promise to take charge of training him."

The boy's face lit up. "Promise, promise, promise!"

My heart soared.

When all the signing was finished, Maryanne pushed back her chair then stood up. "You will be getting frequent unannounced visits from social workers, one being me. First priority, Frank, enroll Brad in school."

Around 5:30, I called my sister Susie, who is a 5th grade school teacher. Her husband Jerry answered the phone. He works in the town's hardware store, which is owned by his uncle, Don. Susie and Jerry own a cottage in town. His widowed mother lives with them and babysits my three-year-old niece, Janet, while Susie works. I asked Jerry if he knew about Brad.

"Susie told me."

"Did she tell you about the puppy?"

"Uh-huh."

"Well, Brad has been sleeping in the washroom with the pup...uhm, Buddy...on the floor, and I wondered if I might borrow that camping mattress of yours until Buddy is trained for long nights without trips outside to relieve himself."

"Pick it up whenever you want, Frank. It's in the garage. In fact, keep it. Things are so hectic around here I don't expect to go camping any time soon. It's just taking up space in the garage."

"Great," I said. "I'll be over to get it. Say, is Susie around?"

"Hold on. Susie? It's Frank!"

I heard the phone change hands and then Susie, "Hey, Frank, what can I do for you?"

"I need you to come over and meet Brad. I'm sure you can figure out what grade he should be enrolled in."

"I'd be glad to. Tomorrow morning?"

"Perfect," I said. Tomorrow morning. Saturday. Susie's day off.

I told Brad about Susie coming over in the morning, that she was my sister, and that she was a teacher. He was to call her Mrs. Warner, not only because she was married to Jerry Warner, but also because Brad would see her at school and Mrs. Warner was what everyone else would be calling her.

CHAPTER SIX

Susie arrived exactly when she said she would. Seeing she brought the camp mattress, I said, "Thanks for bringing that. Brad spent last night on the washroom floor again."

"It will be nice when Buddy is trained to go outdoors," she said.

"According to the book," I said, "making it through the night won't happen for at least another three weeks." I went to the bottom of the stairs and called, "Brad, please come down."

He bounded down the stairs and into the kitchen, Buddy in hot pursuit.

"This is my sister, Mrs. Warner," I said proudly. "She is going to ask you about your schooling."

She smiled at him and clasped his hand. I could see him instantly relax. As we hunkered down at the table, Buddy weaved in and out of our legs. "So Brad," she said, "when was the last day you attended school?"

"Don't remember exactly, but it was when that big tornado wrecked the town I lived in."

"I remember that day," she said.

"I was going to the school the tornado wrecked."

"How awful," she said. "What grade were you?"

"Fifth."

"I hear you have a book on puppy training."

He looked down at the book on his lap.

"How about reading a couple of pages for Frank and me?"

"Sure." He read fairly well.

She handed him a sheet of paper spattered with addition and subtraction equations. "See if you can figure out the answers."

He breezed through that sheet and then a sheet of multiplication and division problems.

"Terrific, Brad," Susie said. "You are up to speed with my students. Frank, enroll Brad in my class."

I winked at Brad. "Susie is the only teacher in Middle who teaches fifth grade."

Suddenly, Buddy began to squat. Brad jumped up then grabbed the puppy and raced outside. The book had taught him the signs that indicated a puppy was about to urinate.

Susie turned to me. "You have a fantastic boy there, Frank."

I flushed with pride. "Wish he was mine."

I was truly thrilled Brad and Buddy were pals. Still I kind of felt like my new pet was not mine to love. One way or the other, I had take over when Brad was in school, but how to keep Buddy safe while I was busy? How long was it going to take for Buddy to know this was home and not to wander off? Might be a good idea to set up a clothesline-type run for Buddy.

That night, Dolly spruced up Brad for Church the next day, giving him a haircut then marching him upstairs to take a shower. She laid out the clothes he had worn the day I first saw him. She had washed and ironed every last stitch. Those clothes looked better than new.

When Brad came out of the bathroom, wearing pajamas, Dolly rushed in, scooped up waterlogged towels and his dirty clothes - clothes her grandson had lent Brad - and charged off to the washing machine. Two outfits were all Brad had for the next few days. Wishing I had more time to shop, I asked, "Have you ever been to Church, Brad?"

He shook his head no.

"Hmm," I muttered, wondering where to start. "First, I guess, you need to know how to bless yourself. Put your right hand on your forehead like this and say, 'In the name of the Father.' Then go down to the middle of your chest like this and say, 'And of the Son.' Then go to one shoulder and over to the other like this, saying, 'And of the Holy Ghost.' And finish up by putting both palms together and say, 'Amen.'"

He scrunched up his face. "That's silly."

"It isn't silly," I said. "Christians do it out of love and respect for the Holy Trinity, which watches over us with every breath we take. Now, I really think you should bless yourself."

He gnawed his bottom lip while inside his head, gears churned. His hand began to move.

I raised my right hand to my forehead. "In the name of the Father."

He did the same.

I dropped my hand to the middle of my chest. "And of the Son."

He did the same.

I touched my left shoulder and then my right. "And of the Holy Ghost."

He did the same.

I put my palms together. "Amen."

And Brad did the same.

I never felt so close to anybody in all my life.

Later that night, I typed the Lord's Prayer on my computer keyboard and printed it out. Bright and early the next morning, I handed Brad a copy then off we went to Saint Timothy's Catholic Church. I had been a fallen away Catholic for the past ten years, much to my family's distress, but I felt I should give Brad a proper religious training. I didn't ask his opinion. It's what all parents do. Imagine that. I was thinking of myself as a parent.

Inside the Church, I whispered instructions, which Brad followed despite looking ill at ease. I understood this was an entirely new situation for him. All the standing and kneeling and sitting aggravated me, too. I wondered if he had ever been told about God. Somehow, I doubted it.

When parishioners went up to the altar to receive Holy Communion, I whispered. "Stay in your seat. You have to get Baptized first then go to Catechism Classes and receive First Communion, get confirmed..."

When he gawked at me as if I was out of my mind, I thought: Holy cow! This parent thing was complicated! Not to mention I was just a bachelor without biological children. What did I know about teaching a child anything?

After Mass, outside the Church, I introduced Father Francis to Brad. Then in the parking lot behind the Church, we ran into my brother Leo and his wife, Heather. I introduced them to Brad then Leo said, "We're going fishing this afternoon. How about joining us?"

"I can't," I said. "I gave two hands the day off and the cows need milking."

Leo faked shock. "Even on Sunday?"

"Even on Sunday," I echoed.

Heather spoke up. "Hey, Brad, would you like to come fishing with us?"

Brad hung his head. "I don't know how to."

"That's okay," she said. "We'll show you."

Leo jabbed me in the ribs. "And Frank will let you borrow his A-number-one fishing rod."

Brad brightened up.

"Okay, okay," I said, waving my hands. "What time will you pick him up?"

"We'll be over at one," Heather said.

"Say, my old bike may be of some use to Brad," Leo said. "We'll bring it when we come."

On the way home, I asked Brad if he ever rode a bike, and of course, the answer was no. I rolled my eyes, thinking, here we go again. I just couldn't picture myself teaching an eleven-year-old how to ride a bike. Sheesh, things were getting harder and harder by the minute.

The second we got home, Brad released Buddy from the run and the two of them charged into the house. I grunted an amused grunt then followed. I heard the phone ring as I opened the kitchen door. It was Leo, calling to let me know that he and Heather decided to pack a lunch, so I was to have Brad hungry when they arrive at 11:45 instead of 1:00. How in the world was I supposed to stop an eleven-year-old from eating? When all I could see of him at that moment was his backside sticking out of the refrigerator? I threw my hands up in the air and headed for my prize fishing rod. While handing it to him, I told him to wait on the back stoop for Leo and Heather. Those cows sorely needed attention.

Totally disregarding my instructions, Brad
- and Buddy - followed me into the barn. "Sure
stinks in here," he said.

"After you've been around here long
enough, you'll get used to it. In fact, it'll become
the smell of home."

Brad twisted up his nose. "I'll never get
used to that smell."

One of the hands by the name of Ron asked,
"Are you teaching the kid to work the farm?"

"I sure am."

Brad's eyes bugged out.

"My siblings and I had to work the farm," I
said. "So should you. Just ask Uncle Leo."

"But you're giving the kid a little time off
before cracking the whip," Ron said. "Is that it?"

"You hit the nail on the head, Ron."

Brad looked apprehensive.

"Don't worry, kid," Ron said. "Frank is a
real nice boss. He really doesn't crack a whip.
Although he's skilled at kicking butts of lazy
hands."

We heard Leo's truck pull into the yard and
his car door slam. Brad ran to the door. "He
brought the bike! Hey, Frank, can I take Buddy to
the lake?"

"You'll have to ask Leo about that," I said
while switching on the milking machines.

CHAPTER SEVEN

As much as I loved working the dairy, I must admit I was green with envy, imagining Leo, Heather, and Brad trucking out to Crystal Lake on this gorgeous Sunday to go fishing. The surface of the water had to be glittering like diamonds. I could just see Brad and Buddy getting out of Leo's truck, whooping it up. Of course, Howie and Tony were there already. I could just hear Leo hollering, "Any bites, Howie?"

"Four bigmouths in fifteen minutes," Howie bragged.

"Gotta come pretty early to get a good ketch," Tony said.

"We had to stop at God's house first," Heather said.

I pictured Leo showing Brad how to bait the line then telling him to take off his shoes and step into the water. That should've been me, not Leo, teaching Brad such things.

So there was Brad, tossing out the line. So as not to get hooked, Leo stood a short distance away and baited his line. Heather had already tossed out her line. And that maniac Buddy was running around, yipping and twirling the way he always did. I could just see the pup bounding into the pristine water then sticking in his snout. He might even bring that snout out of the water then lift it high in the air and sneeze. I imagined him bounding out of the lake then shaking his sweet little body so hard he almost lost his balance.

"I got one!" Heather squealed in my mind's eye. And there was Brad watching her reel in a huge bigmouth bass, watching her unhook it and putting it in the cooler. Inspired, Brad tossed out his line again. A pull on the line, and then Brad did all the things to his fish he had seen Heather do to hers.

Leo caught a big one, too.

What I didn't imagine - and never in a million years could have imagined - was Buddy wandering off into some nearby bushes. Or Brad hearing a yip and looking over at the bushes. Or when yips turned into yelps, Brad stepping out of Crystal Lake, putting down the fishing rod, and going to investigate. All that reality and more, I was to find out in a very short time:

As Brad hurried to the bushes, Howie hollered from upstream, "Hey, your dog's scaring off the fish!"

"What is wrong with you, Buddy?" Brad asked, his hands parting branches. "Come out of there, you silly..." He squinted into the shadows. "Mama? Mama!"

Leo and Heather dropped their rods and raced to the bushes, getting there just as Tony and Howie did. All of them stopped in their tracks. Chucked into the bushes was a body.

Leo snagged onto Brad then hauled him out of the bushes and turned him away. "That's your mother?"

"Y-yes!" Brad shrieked. He yanked free of Leo then ran to the shoreline and collapsed on the sand. He cried so much, everybody was at a loss as to how to comfort him.

Leo speed dialed my cell phone. Thank God, I had it on me. I dropped everything then raced to my truck and headed to Crystal Lake.

Meanwhile, Leo speed dialed our brother John, the Sheriff of Middle. Crystal Lake was located in Swain, a town smaller than Middle. Having no police force of its own, Swain relied on Middle for police assistance. However, John had never dealt with a murder, even though he had the training to deal with it. So before leaving his office, John called his good friend, Sherman, who lived in Oakridge. Sherman had been an MP in the Army and had helped solve several murders.

I arrived at Crystal Lake just as John and Deputy Warren did. I leaped out of my truck and raced to Brad. I felt so helpless. All I could do was to wrap my arms around him and let him cry out his grief. Strange how much he still loved his mother. After the way she mistreated him? After the way she let Jake mistreat the both of them? And what about those cigarette burns?

Leo spoke up, "Looks like the five of us are witnesses to a murder."

I glanced at him and then at Heather. She sent me a perplexed look. "We were told to stay put until investigators have time to do in-depth questioning."

"Wonder how long that'll be," Howie said.

"Hey, look," Tony said. "Here comes John.

Pulling Brad and me aside, John said calmly, "I need to ask Brad some questions."

I held Brad at arm's length and gave him a reassuring nod.

"Okay," Brad said just above a whisper.

"Not counting here today," John said, "when was the last time you saw your mother?"

"The day I met Frank."

"Before or after you met Frank?"

"Before. Mama and Jake were fighting when I woke up."

"Frank told me you're afraid of Jake...uhm...his last name, again?"

"Burke."

"Right. Burke. You're afraid of Jake Burke."

Brad shivered a nod.

"So how was it you ended up on that bench that morning?"

"Jake backhanded Mama and I hollered at him to stop. He looked like a monster twisting around, twisting and twisting, and looking at me with great big monster eyes. I knew right there and then I was in for it real good, so I got out of there. Real fast."

"Do you think Jake Burke did this?"

"He killed Mama!" Brad wailed. "He's a monster! He killed her! I hate him! I hate him!"

I grabbed hold of Brad and held him tight. "It's okay, Brad. Everything's going to be okay."

John yanked out his cell phone and dialed. "Never mind coming here, Sherm. Go see if you can round up a guy named Jake Burke. Cool his heels at my office till I get there. Yeah, Burke's prime suspect. Description? Hold on..." John jammed the cell phone against Brad's cheek. "Tell Sherman what Jake Burke looks like."

After reuniting Brad and me with the other witnesses, John helped Deputy Warren to scour the scene with a fine tooth comb.

Hunkered down on the blanket spread on the ground, I stared at the picnic basket and the pail of the day's catch. There wasn't near as many bigmouth bass in that pail as I had previously imagined. Nor were they as huge as I had previously imagined.

Heather cleared her throat. "We should eat."

The idea of the deceased woman sprawled nearby, plus the boy crying his heart out for his dead mother, wiped out any and all appetites.

Vans rolled onto the scene, bringing police tape and other paraphernalia needed to protect the integrity of the crime scene. One investigator carried a small recorder, making comments into it while inspecting the scene and the body. The Coroner arrived. Shortly thereafter, a bulging black body bag was whisked away.

At long last, John trudged back to us. "You're free to leave. It's likely I'll be contacting one or all of you in the near future, so don't be too surprised." He made eye contact with Brad. "This is a terrible thing to go through, son - for anyone to go through. But I want you to know that if you need anything - anything at all - no matter the hour - don't give a second thought to calling me. Here's my card with my number. I'm so sorry for your loss."

Brad gave John a weak nod. Thankfully, his crying had come to an end.

John's phone rang. "Yeah." He listened. "Good job, Sherm. I'll be there in two shakes of a lamb's tail." He hung up then nodded at us. "Jake Burke's been arrested at the Wildwood Motel and is now in transit to the Middle Jail."

Thirty minutes later, after dropping off Brad into the capable arms of Dolly, I was walking into John's office. Sitting handcuffed in a chair was Jake. "What the hell am I doing here?" Jake bellowed, "I didn't kill nobody!"

"You sure did," I spat. "Brad says you beat his mother all the time. Him, too. You went too far, this time. You killed her."

Jake leered at me. "Who the hell are you? I never seen you before in all my life! And how do you know Brad? Where is he anyhow?"

"None of your business," I growled. "Brad's safe from the likes of you."

"I demand to see him!" Jake hollered.

I crossed my arms and shook my head side to side.

"Damn you! I got rights to that stinking brat!"

"You're never getting your rotten hands on him again," I said.

"Okay, okay, everybody calm down," John said. He squinted at Deputy Warren. "Have you read the suspect Miranda Rights?"

"Not yet."

John looked Jake, square in the eyes and said, "Jake Burke, you are under arrest for the murder of Elsie Lapinski. You have the right to remain silent. Anything you say can and will be used against you in a court of law. You have the right to consult with an attorney. If you can't afford an attorney, the state will provide one at no cost to you. Deputy Warren, empty the contents of Jake Burke's pockets and lock it in the safe. Then put him in the holding cell. County

Prosecutor's on his way. Soon Jake Burke's sorry butt will be hauled out of Middle."

"Good riddance," I said.

John grabbed his hat and chucked it onto his head. "In the meantime, I'm going over to check out the apartment. Most likely, the murder took place there."

"I'm going with you," I said, trailing John out the door. "I want to get Brad's things."

"Don't expect there'll be much," John said.

My fatherly instinct kicked in. "For a boy his age, anything that brings back good memories is better than nothing."

During the thirty-minute drive, I asked. "How's Linda?" I hadn't kept up with John and his family lately. They were expecting their second child. Their first child, Paul, was three years old.

"Bigger than a house," John said.

"So any day now," I said.

He chuckled. "Wish any-day-now was yesterday."

What a dump the apartment was. "How," I wondered aloud, "did Brad manage to become such a nice boy when he was so mistreated and living in a pigsty like this?"

"Gives you cause to wonder," John muttered then went about his business.

I couldn't see anything that might help Brad overcome the murder of his mother. In a bedroom that must have been Brad's, a stuffed monkey lay on the floor beside the bed. It looked its age. I went through the drawers, putting the contents, which included clothes, into the bag I had brought with me. I went over, picked up the monkey, and that filled that bag. I should've brought more bags.

I scanned the room and spotted an old cardboard box. In it were some books and pictures. I picked up the box. There wasn't much more in the apartment to add to it, so I was soon done. "How much longer will you be here?" I asked John.

"Another hour maybe."

"That gives me time to go to Kmart. Brad needs better clothes than I found here. Plus I need a few other things."

"Pick me up a soft drink, will you?"

At Kmart, all the things on the unwritten list in my head went into a shopping cart. Heading for the checkout, I weaved into the electronics section. "Computers. I didn't see one in the apartment. Brad needs to be up with modern kids." So a desk top computer, a tower, and a bunch of other electronic rigmarole ended up in my shopping cart.

Near the checkout, a refrigerator containing soft drinks and beer hummed. "Maybe I should buy a beer instead of a soft drink for John. Nah, he's on duty."

Driving back to the Sheriff's Office, John said, "I found some papers of interest. A couple of them concerned Brad. I have to call Sherm about them. He'll know what to I should do with them. Why don't you bring Brad by my office tomorrow and we'll have a sit-down?"

CHAPTER EIGHT

I came home to such a sad boy, and I could tell that Dolly was putting on a brave face not only for him, but also for me. However, the truth came out a short time later. "Brad has had such an awful life for a child so young," she lamented. "I hope we'll be able to wipe away his tears and give him a normal life. I know folks in Middle will be working on their end. I'm so glad Brad has Buddy to care for and love."

After supper, I headed out the back door to do chores in the barn. "Come with me, Brad. I have some of your things in the truck."

"Really?"

I nodded. "John and I went to the apartment your mother and you were living in. I did my best to pick out your things."

Brad looked uncertain, as if deciding whether he liked me going to that apartment or not.

"I'm considering whether or not to keep you out of school for a few days," I said.

He froze.

I glanced back at him. He was white as a sheet. I went back to him. "What's the matter?"

"What about Jake?"

"Jake Burke is in County Jail by now," I said. "Far away from Middle."

Brad wrung his hands. "Jake won't like it if I go to school."

"He has absolutely no say in the matter," I spouted. "He can't stop you - or anybody - from doing anything anymore."

Brad was in an awful dither. "But he can, Frank! He says he can do anything he wants to!"

"No, he can't, Brad. Listen to me. Jake said stuff like that to scare you. Forget him."

Brad studied me.

I couldn't help but think: Holy smokes, that bastard did one god-awful job on this boy. I took in a deep breath then said, "There's one thing you must know about me, Brad: I am a truthful man. I will never intentionally say or do anything to put you in harm's way - to put anybody in harm's way. So, do you want to go to school tomorrow or not?"

His head jiggled up and down.

"Okay," I said. "Let's get your gear out of the truck."

Next thing I knew, Brad was pulling down the tailgate of my truck and climbing up into the bed. "My monkey!" he shrieked. He held the stuffed animal to his heart, weaving side to side. "Mama gave me Monkey Boy when I was just born!"

After chores, I cleaned up then called Susie to update her on Brad and to tell her he was coming to school in the morning. When she told me the time to expect the school bus at the top of my driveway, I cut her off, "I'm bringing him in myself this week and picking him up. He's at wits end and I want to see him though this transition. He can take the bus next week."

"Good idea," she said. "Be at the school at 8:30. Go straight to the office to enroll him. Now, I don't want you to worry about him, Frank. Everyone at the school will do their best to make him feel welcome. I have spoken to all the teachers and my class about him. Every one of them is going to be very kind to him."

Driving to school the next morning, I said, "My brothers and sisters really liked going to school here. I think you will, too."

"I walked by it, one day," Brad said. "It's kind of small. I always went to big schools."

"Me, too," I said. "But I would've liked going to school here. I got this idea that small schools are better than big city schools."

He sighed. "A kid can get lost in the crowd."

In the Main Office, Principal Raymond Farley met us with a smile and enthusiastic handshakes. "So you're Mrs. Warner's new student," he said to Brad. "Welcome to our school! Now, just to let you know, Mrs. Warner filled out all the necessary forms in advance.

Signatures are needed on a few of them, but then off you go to Room 5!"

"Is it okay if I walk Brad there?" I asked.

"Absolutely!"

As Brad and I navigated the hallway, I whispered, "Weird how quiet halls get when students are in class."

"Yeah," Brad whispered.

We stopped at the door to Room 5. I looked down at him. Those large blue eyes peered up at me. I smiled. "I better knock, huh?" he whispered.

"Yeah," I whispered.

Well, Brad went in, I waved to Susie, and off I went, through the weird quiet hallway. Jumbled emotions overflowed my being.

I picked up Brad after school. "How'd it go?"

He shrugged. "Okay, I guess."

That's all I got out of him. Maybe Susie would call me, I thought, and embellish the day. When I didn't turn for home, he asked, "Where we going?"

"John asked us to stop by."

Two seats occupied the front of John's desk. I took one. Brad took the other. John was sitting behind the desk. "First of all, Brad," he said, "I know this is hard for you, but a burial service is in the works for your mother. The town has a budget for situations like this. It may be tomorrow around this time. Burial will be in the town cemetery."

"I'll have a gravestone made," I said.

The tears started to flow down Brad's cheek.

"Second thing is," John said, "there will be a trial and considering the overwhelming evidence, Jake will be convicted. The State will want you to take the stand, Brad, and tell the court the kind of treatment doled out to you and your mother."

"Can you do that, son?" I asked.

Brad hiccupped through his tears. "Yeah. I can. And I will. Jake can't get away with killing Mama."

"Okay, now," John said. "Time to dry those tears and get over to Abby's This And That. She's anxious to talk to you and see how you are doing. While you are gone, I will be talking to Frank."

"I'll pick you up at the store when I'm done here," I said.

After Brad closed the door, John said, "I found this letter. It was sent to Elsie Lapinski the day Brad was born."

I took the letter from him and read:

Dear Elsie,

You pulled a fast one on me by getting pregnant. Did you really think I am stupid enough to give up my life for you and a kid? You will never see me again. However, I am sucker enough to think I should pay you child support. You will get $1200 from me every month until the kid is eighteen. Be sure to let my solicitors know if you move.

You have to do two things. One, tell no one I am the father. Two, take care of the kid until it is eighteen.

Do not think for one minute that if the kid dies or if you give him up for adoption, I won't know. My detectives will be keeping track of you and the kid. Goodbye forever,
William Campbell

"So now we know why Jake wanted to get his hands on Brad," I said. "He wanted to get his grubby paws on that monthly check William was sending."

"Ask Lisa to contact William Campbell and tell him about Elsie's death," John said. "Campbell needs to know you are now Brad's guardian."

"I don't want his money," I said.

"Lisa might be able to get Campbell to sign papers giving up paternal claims," John said.

"I'll call her as soon as I get home," I said.

"Burial could be as early as tomorrow," John said.

"Let me know when you know for sure," I said.

CHAPTER NINE

When we got back to the farm, Brad and Buddy reunited, acting like they had not seen each other in a hundred years. I shuddered to think of that boy without his puppy. How could I alone ever get him through all the trauma? Yes, that puppy, a family, and friends were just what the doctor ordered.

They remained outside, goofing around, while I went into the kitchen. After I filled in Dolly about the afternoon's events, she said, "Shelby and I will be going to the funeral service."

"I'll let you know what time it will be as soon as John lets me know," I said.

"Well, I'm heading home now," she said, slinging her pocketbook over her shoulder.

"See you tomorrow," I said, picking up the phone.

I dialed Lisa. After bringing her up to date, I asked her to contact William Campbell about Elsie Lapinski's death and let him know Brad was with me. "Do you think Campbell would sign away his paternal rights to Brad?"

"Hard to say," Lisa said. "I'll do my best to make it happen."

"I know you will," I said. "Sometimes I think I ask too much of you and the rest of the family."

"That's what families do," Lisa said. "Speaking of families, you should have a family get-together to welcome Brad."

"Good idea," I said. "I'll work on that."

Later on, John called. "The funeral is tomorrow morning at ten."

"Which means Brad has to miss a day of school his first week," I grumbled. "When is he ever going to have some normalcy in his life?"

I called Susie and told her Brad would not be in school tomorrow. Then I called everyone else about the time.

Next morning, shortly after nine, Brad and I met John in his office. Doc Stone came in to speak to Brad. As in most small towns, Doctor Barry Stone maintained a facility that served as a temporary morgue. "Would you like one last look at your mother before I close up the casket?"

Brad's face went snow white. He choked on his response, so I spoke up, "I'll go with you."

We followed Doc to the morgue. Elsie Lapinski looked okay, like she was just sleeping. Brad put his hand on her cheek. Once again, tears overflowed his eyes. Oh, how I hated seeing him cry. "Goodbye Mama," he murmured.

Doc Stone reached for the lid of the casket and lowered it.

Brad stepped back against me.

I wrapped my arms around him and we stood there, staring at the closed casket.

After a while, Brad and I along with John, Leo, Joey, and Susie's husband Jerry picked up the casket and took it outside where the town's ambulance, which doubled as a hearse, waited. We loaded the casket into the hearse then Brad and I followed John to his unmarked car and got in. Leo, Joey, and Jerry got into Leo's car. The hearse pulled away from the curb and headed to the cemetery, John and Leo's cars right behind it.

Father Francis from Saint Timothy's was waiting at the cemetery. Dolly, Shelby, Heather, Susie, Abby, even Maryanne Reardon, the social worker, were there. Many other townsfolk turned out, showing support to Middle's newest citizen in his time of grief. I have never been prouder of all these people.

We pallbearers carried the casket to the open gravesite then set it next to the opening.

"Please joins hands," Father Francis said. "Let us pray. Dear, Lord, accept the soul of Elsie Lapinski."

We lowered the casket into the ground and then covered it with earth. One by one, people offered condolences to Brad and told him they were his friends and to call them anytime. I could tell Brad felt comforted. Their kindness certainly overwhelmed me.

Walking to John's unmarked car, I told Brad, "The gravestone I ordered will be set in place in a day or so."

"Can we come and see it?" he asked.

I nodded. "We'll bring flowers."

"Daisies," he said. "Mama used to pick wild daisies whenever she saw some beside the road."

At John's office, Brad and I got into my truck and headed home. The ride was quiet. I glanced at Brad. "A penny for your thoughts."

"Isn't it impolite to call a priest by his first name?" he asked.

I chuckled. "Francis is Father's last name. His first name is Martin. However, at some Churches, parishioners do call their priests by their first names."

"It's kind of friendly," Brad said.

"It is friendly," I said. "Did you know that my name is really Francis?"

Brad raised an eyebrow at me.

"Yup, Francis," I said. "But I've always gone by the nickname, Frank.

"Frank Brendan," he said. "Nice name."

"Remember when we signed all those papers, so you could legally stay at my place?"

"Uh-huh."

"Well, since then, I've been thinking of you as my son. Is it all right with you if I adopt you?"

"Adopt me?"

"That way your last name will change to Brendan," I said.

Brad got really upset. "Mama won't like that at all!"

I felt like a darn fool for asking him such a thing on the very day of his mother's burial. "Okay," I said. "That's fine."

"If you adopt me can I stay Brad Lapinski?"

I sighed. "Sure."

On Saturday, Lisa, Susie, and Maryanne Reardon came to consult with me about Brad. Lisa outlined her meeting with William Campbell: "Brad dodged the bullet when his father didn't want him. That man is *crud*! He's only too happy to sign a quit-claim to his son. Here is a copy for you and one for Maryanne. The original is in my file."

"Are you planning to adopt Brad or keep him as a Foster Child?" Maryanne asked. "If he stays a Foster Child, the State will pay you a monthly stipend."

"I don't want any money," I said. "I'd rather adopt him. Is it necessary to change his name?" I told them about Brad's response to changing his name. "Why do you think he's so against it?"

"His mother - and more than likely, Jake, too - was paranoid about losing the monthly stipend from William Campbell," Lisa said.

"One - or both of them - must have said something to Brad about always staying his mother's child," Susie said.

Maryanne Reardon nodded. "Children, when they are very young, are programmed with lots of do's and don'ts. Children take on parental programming as forever the truth, often never learning that there comes a time when what they were told is no longer true."

"They also take words literally," Susie said. "If you tell a child he is going to be 'blown away', he expects a big wind to come along and blow him into the next town."

"Bottom line, Frank," Lisa said. "Adoptions can be done without name changes."

"Perhaps as he gets older, he'll want to change his name," Susie said.

"I suppose so," I said. "How is Brad doing in school?"

"Well, he's only been in my class a couple of days," Susie said. "But at first glance, I'd say he is very sad and standoffish, which is to be expected. He does the work okay. Still, my heart bleeds for him. He has the weight of the world on his shoulders."

Maryanne spoke up, "He needs to see a counselor."

Susie spoke up, "Father Francis is a counselor. Before he became a priest, he was a psychologist."

"I'll see to it that Brad visits Father Francis." I turned to Lisa. "How soon can you start the adoption process?"

"Within the next three weeks."

"One way or the other, I want to give him a welcome party," I said.

"You should discuss that with Father Francis," Susie said.

"I agree," Maryanne said. "Brad is very fragile."

Lisa poked me. "And he may find it hard to deal with such a crowd."

I chuckled. "I'll check it out with Father before I do anything. All I can say is: Thank God I have so many of you to help me with my son-to-be. More and more, I find I am ill-equipped to handle this boy who has so many giant problems to deal with."

Before Lisa, Maryanne and Susie left, they wanted to say hi to Brad. They found him in the barn - with Buddy.

At supper, I told Brad that I was going to speak to Father on Sunday after Mass, about counseling sessions. "Talking will help you get use to your new life here with me."

Brad appeared agitated.

"Father Francis is a kind and caring man," I said. "I'm sure you'll enjoy talking with him."

So after Sunday Mass, Brad and I spoke to Father Francis. "Counseling sessions are a wise thing to do. I'm pleased and honored that you thought of me to do them. Do you know I have a degree in psychology?"

"Susie told me," I said.

Glancing at his calendar, Father Francis said, "Let me see now. Hmm... Looks like I can see Brad after school on Monday, Wednesday and Friday. Now listen to me, Brad, you need to know that anything said between you and me is private. I will never tell anyone - not even Frank - so you need not fear that. But you can if you want to."

I spoke up, "I promise never to ask or force you to tell me anything."

CHAPTER TEN

A month later, Brad and I were in court with Lisa, finalizing the adoption. Maryanne and Dolly were there, too. Lisa put forms in front of the Judge. He signed them then turned to Brad. "Mr. Lapinski, you are aware that Frank Brendan is now and forever your father?"

"Yes, sir."

"And Mr. Brendon has promised to love and care for you for the rest of your life?"

"Yes, sir."

"It would be nice if you return that love and caring."

"Yes, sir."

After court, we ate at the finest restaurant in Oakridge. I kept looking at the adoption papers, over and over again, my heart bursting with happiness. I thought I would never have a son. I sent Brad a smile that nearly broke my face. He looked just as pleased.

Maryanne handed me Brad's birth certificate, which she had been kind enough to pick up at the courthouse. "My son was born February 23, 1989," I said. "We will always celebrate his birthday on Feb. 23rd, but today's date, May 17, 2000, is a special day, too, so we shall always celebrate this date, too. Let's lift our glasses and declare both days joyful days. Come on, Brad, lift your glass, too!"

Brad grinned through his surprise. As glasses clinked, I could read his mind: People actually think that having him in their lives was something to be joyful about?

When we got up to leave Maryanne said, "Brad, this is goodbye for now, but know that I will always be your friend. I'd be happy to hear from you from time to time."

Upon arriving home, I noticed the answering machine blinking. I clicked it on. It was Mom asking me to call her. I did and got some bad news that spoiled the, so far, terrific day: Nanny died. She was eighty-two years old and sick, so it wasn't entirely unexpected. There was going to be a service for her in Texas with all her friends. Afterward, Mom and Dad planned to accompany the casket to Middle for a service with family and friends. Nanny was to be buried beside Poppy.

"I need you to make arrangements at Saint Timothy's for Wednesday, May 20th," Mom said.

"I'll take care of it," I said. "I'll plan a catered reception afterwards. It'll be too much for Dolly to take on. Now, don't worry about things on this end, Mom. I'll let everyone around here know about Nanny and the arrangements."

CHAPTER ELEVEN

Mom gave Brad a big hug, much to his shock and distress. Though he smiled bravely, I think he secretly enjoyed it. Nobody else but Mom could get away with that.

Dad wouldn't dream of hugging Brad; although, he acted as if he felt like doing just that. He merely took Brad by the hand and shook it. "Welcome to the family, Brad. It's terrific to see Frank has a fine son like you."

The biggest grin swept over Brad, the biggest I had ever seen on him. If he was trying to hold back, he didn't succeed.

Dolly and I figured that Nanny's funeral and the following reception might be too much for Brad to handle so soon after his mother's funeral. So, now that Brad was riding his bike into town on occasion, Dolly arranged for him to bike to Shelby's house, where he and Jason could spend the day. It warmed my heart to see Brad and Dolly's grandson become friends.

Sunday, after the funeral, I asked Mom and Dad, "Will you be moving back here now that Nanny's gone?"

"It's been nice being with family..." Mom began.

Dad cut in, "But we enjoy Texas weather and the seashore. We have friends there. So no, we're staying put."

"But we plan to vacation here," Mom added quickly.

"Plus, these days, keeping in touch by phone and e-mail is a cinch," Dad said.

"So how much longer are you staying?" I asked.

Dad and Mom exchanged confused glances. "Two more weeks?" he stammered.

"Is that okay?" Mom asked.

"Yes. Yes, of course it is," I stammered. "It's only that...well...Brad has to go to court next week as a witness against Jake Burke and..."

Mom gasped. "The man who killed his mother?"

I nodded.

"That's much too much for that little boy!" she insisted. "If I were you, I would not allow it!"

"Mom, Brad wants to do this. Jake beat him and his mother and ended up killing her. Brad has never had the power to fight back, but now he does - and he knows it. He wouldn't miss this for anything, and I won't stop him."

It's weird how anxious Brad was about going to court. As Mom, Dad, Brad, and I walked into the Court House, Lisa was talking to the District Attorney. "I am Albert Denny, lead

Prosecutor in the Elsie Lapinski murder case. I'm
having Mr. Lapinski and his father wait in the
Witness Room. That court officer over there..."
He pointed to a young man with red hair and
freckles. "His name is Mr. Hogan. He will come
and get you when it's time for you to take the
stand. Mr. Hogan will lead you into the
courtroom. He will direct you, Mr. Brendon, to
take a seat in the gallery with your parents. Mr.
Hogan will then open the gate to the witness
stand where Brad Lipinski will give testimony."

    As we sat in the Witness Room, Brad kept
getting up and sitting down, itching to get going.
An eternity seemed to pass before that door
opened and Mr. Hogan said, "It's time."

    I had never been in a courtroom before.
This one was a lot smaller than I expected. Jake
Burke was sitting at the Defense Table with his
Court-appointed Attorney. Jake was wearing a
nicely-tailored suit, more than likely the best he
ever wore, if indeed, he had ever worn a suit at
all. The hateful look on his face hadn't changed
though. Neither had his temperament. "That kid
can't be a witness against me! He's just a stupid
little boy!"

    The Judge slammed his gavel on the bench.
"I will have quiet in my courtroom! Anyone
disrupting proceedings will be held in contempt!"

    I took a seat beside my parents as Brad
took the stand. He told the court his full name

and then swore to tell the truth. Prosecutor Denny began, "Mr. Lapinski, do you know Jake Burke?"

"Yes," Brad replied.

"Is Jake Burke in the Court Room, today?"

"Yes."

"Please point him out for the Court."

Brad's finger aimed straight at Jake Burke who twisted up his face and growled like a rabid dog.

The Judge slammed his gavel on the bench. "One more outburst from the Defendant and I'll have the Bailiff remand the Defendant to the Video Room where he will watch the proceedings in solitary. Continue, Mr. Denny."

"Yes, Your Honor. Mr. Lapinski, tell the jury what Jake Burke was like when he lived with you and your mother, the late Elsie Lapinski."

"Jake never worked. He just sat there in the old chair outside the back door and drank. Mom tried to find work all the time. When she wasn't looking, Jake stole money out of her pocketbook and snuck off to buy booze and hits."

"By 'hits', do you mean drugs?"

"Yes. Pills. Plastic bags of marijuana. Jake made stinky cigarettes out of that stuff. He got real mad if Mom didn't have any money and then he beat her up. I tried to make him stop, but then he beat me up, too."

Jake's attorney didn't cross-examine Brad. The evidence was too overwhelming. Weeks later, I ran into him in Middle. In confidence, he told me, "I don't believe that little boy should have to suffer through any more indignity at the hands of Jake Burke."

At lunch, Lisa told Brad, "I want you to call me Aunt Lisa from now on. Here's my card with my phone number at the office. I wrote my cell phone number on it, too, and my home e-mail address. Get in touch with me, okay?"

Brad smiled at her and nodded.

Mom took Dad's hand and with a twinkle in her eye, she said to Brad, "It will make our day if you call us Nanny and Poppy."

I was thinking it would make my day if Brad called me Dad, but I was too afraid to ask.

As we parted ways, I asked Lisa to let Brad and I know the verdict as soon as she knows. No sooner did we reach the driveway to the farm when my cell rang. It was Lisa. The jury found Jake Burke guilty of murdering Elsie Lapinski.

CHAPTER TWELVE

Brad's training of Buddy was going real well. Dolly did a lot toward that goal. I wasn't doing much; my chores in the barn bogged me down. I felt pretty guilty. Thankfully, Dad pitched in while Mom helped Dolly in the house. Meals were awesome.

Brad was now calling my parents, Nanny and Poppy. I was jealous. I wanted to be called Dad. I wondered if it would ever happen.

Lisa called the week after the jury came back with a guilty verdict. "The judge sentenced Jake to life without parole."

"Brad will be happy to hear that," I said.

"How's Mom and Dad?"

"Happy as roosters at dawn," I said.

"Huh?"

"Brad's calling them Nanny and Poppy now," I said.

"Oh."

"If he called me Dad, now, that would be great."

"Did you ask him to?"

I heaved a sigh. "No. I figured I should let him decide on that."

"You're a donkey." Lisa said.

"You used to call me an ass," I said.

"I'm a polite attorney now."

"So...why am I a donkey?"

"Brad's a kid. Tell him to call you Dad."

After hanging up, I went outside to find Brad. He and Buddy were in the barn with the hands who were teaching him about the cows. He seemed interested and eager to help. I cleared my throat, loudly, to let them know I was there. Then I said, "Jake got life without parole."

Brad let out a gush of air. "Harrah!" He started running around, Buddy jouncing along side of him. Suddenly, Brad stopped. "Can I call Jason, Frank, and tell him about it?"

"Only if you called me Dad instead of Frank."

Brad lit up like a light bulb. "You'll let me? Is it okay?"

"Of course, it's okay. I'm your father, for Pete's sake!"

"Okay, *Dad.*"

Dolly and I were in the kitchen. Brad was outside with Buddy, Brad on one end of a stick, Buddy on the other end. "Listen to that boy laugh," Dolly said, stepping to the window. "I never heard Brad laugh at all, never mind like he's doing right now."

Basking in that glorious sound, I said, "Amazing isn't it?"

"Yeah," she said. "You really have to get working on that big get-together to officially welcome him."

"Brad's been meeting with Father Francis for several weeks and..."

Dolly cut me off, "Brad is ready."

The next morning, I stopped by the Rectory. It was eleven o'clock. Father Francis was on his way out. "I should have called first," I said.

He waved me off. "Walk me to my car."

"Tell me," I said. "Is Brad adjusting well enough to deal with the big party I'd like to throw for him? He calls me Dad now and laughs a lot lately; and I don't think he's faking."

"Brad is coming along fine in my estimation. A party will certainly help to cement any feeling he might have about belonging not only to a family, but also to a community. I'd say: Go ahead; give a party."

So I told Brad about it. His eyes bugged out. "A party? For me?"

I nodded. "I want the whole world to know you are my son."

"When?"

"Saturday, May 30th, Memorial Day weekend. Rain date is the next day."

To say he was thrilled was an understatement. He whopped and hollered, so loud he scared the bageebees out of Buddy.

Mom and Dad were tickled pink. "We'll still be here!"

I held a meeting the next evening. I wanted everyone's involvement. I was going to provide lots of snacks, coffee, soft drinks, beer, and wine. Susie was in charge of inviting relatives plus the entire Middle citizenry. Jerry was going to borrow the gigantic grill from the Knights of Columbus of which we were members. He would make sure Dad, the grill king, had plenty of charcoal.

"I'll rent a giant tent, tables and chairs, refrigerators, and coolers for food and drink, etc.," Lisa said. "Oh, and the port-a-potties."

"This And That will supply all the paper dishes, napkins, and utensils," Abby said.

Shelby was a camera buff and so was Carol Panouski. We were going to get lots of photos, that's for sure.

John volunteered to bring hot dogs and hamburgers, rolls, condiments, and chips. He said Deputy Warren was going to take charge of traffic control.

Marinated steak tips and chicken had always been Joey's specialty, so it was understood he was taking care of that.

"I'm head honcho of games," Leo said. "I'll set up volleyball, crochet, and horseshoes."

"Make sure there's plenty of bats and balls for baseball," I said.

Mom planned to make potato salad, cold slaw and a garden salad. She promised to whip up her world-famous salad dressings.

Dolly was going to bake breads and desserts.

Father Francis had the job of praying for good weather.

The next night, Charles Woodward called to say he was furnishing a pig and a rotisserie. He would bring it over first thing the morning of the party and take complete charge of it. That wasn't the only thing that blew my mind. Must've been at least twenty of the men in town who said they would lend a hand.

The big day came. We lucked out; what beautiful weather!

The rental truck pulled in at eight o'clock. Three men got out and went right to work setting up all they brought. The town volunteers arrived and pitched right in. Brad and Dad were so lost in the mix that Buddy couldn't keep track of them, so he kept barking and racing around. A real nuisance, but he was entertaining.

Charlie got the pig set up in the rotisserie. Too soon, the aroma made my mouth water.

Mom and Dolly had made sure that Brad had new jeans and new shirt. After all, he was the special person of the day.

Guest started arriving at ten o'clock. I had a dessert table set up and they put their goodies on it. Most of them ended up at the rotisserie, drooling over the sizzling pork.

At eleven o'clock, Brad and I stood on a wooden platform I had constructed. I placed my hand on his shoulder and crowed, "Ladies and Gentlemen! Brothers and Sisters! Moms and Dads! Let me introduce my son Brad! This Gala is to show you how happy he has made me. Now, all of you! Please welcome my son to Middle and enjoy the food and games!"

At one o'clock, Dad's grill was hot and full steam ahead. Hamburg. Hotdogs. Steak tips. Chicken. Nobody had to be called to get food - the aromas did that. Most people needed two plates to accommodate their share of food. Everyone was stuffed. Incredibly, the table of sweets dwindled down to nothing.

The games continued into the night. Nobody seemed to want to go home. When they did, they bubbled over with all the fun they had and that the town should get together every Memorial Day from now on! They taunted Brad about it: "Is it all right with you if we have a 'Welcome Party for Brad every year?"

He didn't need to reply, his beaming face gave the answer.

CHAPTER THIRTEEN

So my life with my son carried on and every year Middle put on a Memorial Day weekend gala. He made many good friends at school, although Jason was his very best friend. Wherever Brad went, Buddy and Jason went, too. They were modern kids and therefore, computer whizzes. When I had questions about my computer, I went to Brad.

He still had a bike, a new one with extra gears; a vast improvement from that old bike Leo gave him. He had a cell phone, too, that was so well used it should have had gray hair. Since he was a good student, I had no hesitation when it came to getting him a guitar. Like all teenagers, he visualized himself and Jason becoming rock stars. Their band was far from being the best; however, they had a blast making a lot of what I considered noise. I hoped this phase would be over and done with before I went deaf.

When Brad was seventeen, he entered eleventh grade. One day, after school, he handed a form to me. "What's this?" I asked.

"Your signature goes at the bottom," he said.

"Not until I know what I'm signing."

"It's for the ROTC program, Dad."

My eyebrows shot to my hairline as I gawked at him. "I had no idea you were interested in the military."

"All the guys - Jason, Tom, Jim - they're all joining the Army. I'm no wimp. I'm joining."

I tapped my index finger on my upper lip. "I'm not going to win this discussion, am I?"

Brad twisted up one side of his face, his head waving side to side. "Here's the rest of the info."

I scanned the ROTC programs. "I expected to send you to college."

He quickly said, "If you want, I'll do the Non-scholarship Program."

"It's not up to me, son. It's your decision."

"I'll go to Oklahoma University for two years then serve three years Active Duty and five years in Inactive Reserves. I get three hundred dollars a month all the way to the end. I intend to do the Officers Training Course along with an Agriculture Course."

He had put a lot of logic into this, but... I swallowed hard then signed the form.

At graduation, the ROTC crew sat together. I was so proud of Brad - of all of those young people. Though patriotic, most were interested in getting the scholarships since college lay beyond most of their means.

CHAPTER FOURTEEN

So there I was, a thirty-six-year farmer, never married, an adopted son in college, and then I received this letter from a teenage girlfriend of long ago.

Frank Brendan
220 E. Whitewash Rd.
P.O. Box 324
Middle, Oklahoma 24382

March 20, 2009

Dear Frank,

I still remember to this day the moment you told me you were leaving Providence to go with your parents, brothers, and sisters to take over your grandparent's farm in Oklahoma. It was quite a shock to me as I was so sure that you and I were deeply in love and would eventually be married. However, I understood how you felt about going with your family. It was something you had to do. There were no choices in the matter.

We did keep in touch - at first - but it wasn't till you were gone for two months and I graduated from high school that I realized I was pregnant with your child. I had started dating Hal Farmer, an Army man, such a wonderful man that I just had to be up front and honest about the baby I was carrying. He loved me, he told me, and well, I loved him back. So when I was five months along, Hal and I married.

We and our little girl, Sky, traveled a lot. To my - and Hal's - disappointment, we had no other children; and so we poured all our devotion onto our wonderful little girl.

Two years ago, Hal was killed in action. Sky and I were devastated. I thought we would never get over losing him. Now, my poor little Sky has more sorrow coming her way. You see, I have cancer. Doctors say I don't have long to live.

Sky has no one but me. My parents, as you know, are missionaries and are now in Africa. There is no way she can go to live with them - and I don't want her to. I am so terrified that if she did go there, she would just languish in her grief - suffer and die from it all.

Please, Frank, take Sky to live with you. I remember how wonderful your entire family was. Give her the love she needs, Frank. Let her become a member of your big family. I know the best place for her to be is with you.

My next door neighbor, Bernice Manning, has your name, address, and phone number. She will guide Sky in my last rites and closing up the house, etc.

I've told Sky that I'm dying and about my last wish for her to go to live with you, her biological father. She is thrown off balance by all this as I am sure you must be, but I feel deep down in my soul that neither one of you will ever regret this.

I am enclosing Sky's birth certificate and a current picture of her. Isn't she beautiful?
All my love,
Marie

What a shock! I had a teenage daughter? Well, you could've bowled me over with a feather! Back when I took in Brad I believed he was to be my only child. Now I have a biological child? I gawked at her birth certificate. On December 3, 1993, Sky Farmer was born in Saint Joseph's Hospital in Providence, Rhode Island. Parents were Hal and Marie Farmer.

I squinted at her picture. She didn't look like me at all, although she could have been Marie's twin - the Marie I had dated long ago. The same infectious smile. The same russet-colored hair. The same leaf green eyes. Bet right now, neither of them is smiling that terrific smile.

I paced the kitchen. When I pick her up at the airport, I'll have no trouble recognizing her. "When I pick her up?" I ran my hand through my hair. "She might not want to come here." I started pacing again. "It's got to be scary to have your mother die and get shipped off to a father you've never seen. I should send her my picture and a long letter introducing myself. I'll give her my e-mail address." I sank onto one of the kitchen chairs. "What if she won't write to me?"

I gawked at Marie's letter. "What about Brad? What do I tell him?" He was in his second year at Oklahoma University. Now and then we got to see each other, but now he's coming home for a month. Then as a lieutenant, he's off to do three years Active Service.

I went into my office, thinking, Marie's letter would have to speak for itself. I scanned it then emailed it to Brad, Mom and Dad, and my siblings. I sat there, mulling over whether or not to call Marie. After a while I made up my mind. I picked up the phone and dialed. Ringing on the other end of the line... I should hang up... "Hello?" said a soft voice."

I choked out, "Hi. Is this...Sky?"

"Who's this?"

"Frank Brendon. Can I speak to your mother?"

Sky started sobbing. "They...just took her... to the hospital."

Moisture filled my eyes. "I'm so, so sorry, Sky. Sky? Are you still there?"

I heard the phone shifting from one hand to another and then, "This is Bernice Manning."

"I'm Frank Brendon. I was thinking about coming to Providence and..."

"No, Frank. It's best if we follow Marie's wishes." Bernice Manning was crying now. "I'll contact you when it's time for Sky to come to you."

A couple days later, I called to see how things were going. Bernice told me Marie died the night of my first call. The funeral was to be in two days. I asked if I could help with expenses and was told no, the insurance Marie had more than covered expenses. I felt so helpless.

I called again the next week. Sky answered, but upon hearing my voice, handed it to Bernice. Sky was going to continue living with Bernice and going to school until the house and furniture sold.

I wrote a long letter to Sky and enclosed a picture of me, Brad, and Buddy. I felt like I wasn't helping her enough to get through this trying time.

On April third, Bernice called me. The house and furniture were sold and she had a bank check, $170,000, made out to Sky Farmer. "I'll give it to her at the airport on April 23. I'll let you know what time to pick her up at the airport there in Oklahoma."

I was astonished that Marie was able to accumulate so much money. It will go a long way toward helping Sky get on with life.

I felt that Bernice Manning deserved compensation for all her help. I talked it over with Lisa. We never did come to a conclusion on that issue, but no matter, the real reason I wanted to talk to Lisa was to ask her whether or not I should hug Sky when I first meet her. "You have good instincts," Lisa said. "They will guide you when the moment comes."

"Dealing with Sky is as scary as dealing with Brad when I first met him," I said. "Then again, Buddy is going crazy missing Brad. Maybe that dog will come through for us again."

"I have no doubt whatsoever about that," Lisa said. "Buddy is going to make Sky feel right at home."

While waiting for the plane to come in, I was as nervous as a groom waiting for his bride to come down the aisle. I imagined Sky was as nervous as I was.

As soon as I saw that sweet forlorn darling, my heart went out to her. I could do nothing less than hug her. I could tell she welcomed the hug, but then she broke down and cried. We sat down on a bench. I took out my handkerchief - the fresh clean one Dolly had stuffed into my pocket when I was leaving for the airport. Wiping away her tears, I said, "There, there, honey, let it all out. It's been a long haul for you."

We picked up her suitcases at the luggage carousel and then headed to the parking garage. "It's good you sent me that picture," Sky said. "I recognized you right away. Your son Brad looks like a nice kid."

I chuckled. "I put that picture in the letter to you at the last minute. It's the latest picture I had of myself. Brad was thirteen when it was taken. He's in college now."

"He's changed quite a bit?" she asked.

"Oh, yeah," I said. "A stunning young man now, if I do say so myself. Wish I could say the same about me. Look at all this grey hair and this embarrassing ponch."

"You look okay to me," she said.

That made me feel good. "Buddy, the dog in that picture, is full grown now, as you will see. Brad is coming home this weekend, for a month, and then he's off to active duty in the Army."

Sky said, "Is Brad my brother?"

"Legally. He's my adopted son. He's born of other parents, but you're my daughter by blood."

I had brought Buddy with me. I figured it wouldn't hurt, and it didn't. I had to shove him over when I got into the driver's seat. When Sky got in, he was squashed in the middle of us. He rested his head on her lap; and she spent the entire trip home, stoking his golden mane. He was in his glory. She was almost as good as Brad.

Dolly was anxiously awaiting our arrival. She had prepared a terrific supper. The three of us sitting down to eat together should have been uncomfortable, but Sky was amazingly open, telling us how wonderful her mother had been, calming everyone while she was the one suffering and dying.

"I wish I could have been there to help," I said.

"Mother knew what was best," Sky said. "She told me about you. She could not keep it from me forever. I'm okay being here."

"You inherited you mother's ability to make others relax and be comfortable," Dolly said.

Sky insisted on helping to clean up after supper while I brought the suitcases up to her room. The boxes of Sky's belongings, which Bernice had shipped via UPS, were stacked up at the bottom of the bed.

"Is it all right if I call Bernice?"

"Anytime," I said. I handed her the latest cell phone on the market. "I bought this for you. The contract covers long distance and unlimited minutes."

Her jaw dropped. "Gee, thanks." Suddenly, she gave me a giant bear hug.

I sat in the living room, staring up at the ceiling, listening to Sky rustling around her room.

Then all was quiet. My very own daughter was asleep up there.

CHAPTER FIFTEEN

I spent Thursday enrolling Sky in Oakridge High School. She wouldn't be starting classes until Monday, so I showed her around Middle on Friday. I introduced her to John and Joey at their respective offices then took her into This And That to meet Abby. We had lunch next door at Louie's Pizza and Sub Shop. After that, we dropped in to visit with Leo and Heather and two of their children, Barry, five years old and Donald, ten months old. Their ten-year-old twins, Jill and Judy, and nine-year-old Chris were in school. Leo and Heather were very busy at their farm as it is well into planting season. It felt so nice squiring my daughter around the town.

Mom and Dad had left Texas this morning, driving up to see their fifteen grandchildren of which Sky was the fifteenth. They were due in on Saturday, the same day Brad was to arrive. All of us were looking forward to the reunion, even Sky.

I had purchased an old but good Buick for Brad to get around in, and since he would be leaving it here when he went off to Active Duty, Sky was going to use it to get back and forth to school and do other things.

Intending to stay the weekend, Lisa came, baggage and cat carrier in hand. And she brought cream puffs! Brad's favorite! Aunt Lisa couldn't wait to see her nephew and to meet her new niece. She had always called him her favorite boyfriend, just to fluster him.

Buddy and I picked up Brad at the bus stop. He looked so great! I nearly broke his back with a bear hug! Though his hair had been hacked to the scalp, he had the makings of a fine mustache. My blond, curly-haired boy was now a man.

Crossing the boundary into the farm, I honked the horn, continuing to do so until reaching the house. Lisa rushed out, shrieking and waving her arms. The rest of the gang traipsing about the old homestead did just about the same. Growing envious of all the hugs, the slaps on the back, whatever, I kind of felt I was just an old dog bone to these people.

Sky was impressed by Brad, I could tell. Who could blame her? The six-foot-two soldier was awesome to look at. A rare blush painted her cheeks. Was she wondering what it might feel like to kiss him? Did she have butterflies in her stomach? Was it love at first sight? I took a step back, chastising myself for having such thoughts.

I took her by the hand. Feeling like Moses parting the sea, I parted the crowd and made our way to Brad. I pulled Sky in front of me. "Brad,

this is Sky. Be nice to her. This means no fighting
like my siblings and I did."

Sky giggled.

"I'm sure we can manage to behave
ourselves, Dad." He winked at her. "But looking
at this beauty, it's likely I'll kiss her before
fighting her."

Dolly swiped away a sentimental tear.
"Food's awaiting. I know that's what Brad and
the rest of you people came all this way for."

Father Francis dropped by. He and Brad
had struck up a lifetime friendship during
counseling days of long ago.

"Stay as long as you can put up with all the
noise and confusion," I said. "Have you ever seen
so many little ones and yakking adults?"

"I had quieter drill sergeants," Brad said.

"I don't know how long I can stand it
myself," I said.

Nanny and Poppy arrived at four o'clock.
Funny how Sky watched Brad and Buddy race
out to greet them; almost like she expected the
same hugs, the same jumping about, the same
barking, the same tom-foolery for herself. To her
surprise, she got it all.

Brad was anxious to go out to the barn to
see the cows. Buddy went with him. So did Sky.
Brad had learned a lot at Oklahoma University
and was thrilled that Sky loved the cows as if
they were beloved pets. I never saw anybody

dote over cows the way she did. She stroked them, she baby-talked them, she patted them, and worried endlessly about the suction cups hurting their teats. I had to continually reassure her that if those cows were not milked, their bulging udders would hurt them a lot more.

At first, Sky didn't like drinking whole milk. So I chilled it to near icing. She tolerated that a lot better. She loved the cream, however, especially the butter, ice cream, and whipped cream Dolly made. She nagged until Dolly gave in and demonstrated the recipes. They ended up making more than enough for this homecoming.

The seven of us: Lisa, Mom, Dad, Sky, Brad, Dolly, and I, sat down for supper. How wonderful to see the kitchen table crowded again. I said Grace, issuing up thanks to the Man Upstairs for all the blessing in my life. After that, Brad and Sky were asked so many questions that I couldn't get in a word edgewise.

When everyone else turned in for the night, Brad and I finally got in quiet talk. "Don't get me wrong, Dad," he said. "You're a handsome man and all, but Sky is over-the-top gorgeous!"

"She doesn't take after me," I said. "That's for sure."

"Did you see those highlights of red in her hair?" he raved. "And those green eyes! I never saw such green eyes!"

"She looks like her mother," I said.

"Bet Sky is prettier!" he exclaimed. "I swear I'm already in love with her! Is there something wrong with me being in love with her, Dad? After all, she is your daughter and I am your son and..."

I cut him off, "Don't you think you're jumping the gun? You really don't know her yet."

"I got a whole month to do that, Dad."

I changed the subject, "Why don't we talk about what you learned at the University?"

Brad gave me a look. After a moment, he said, "Oh, all right. Well, let's see... You buy cows whenever you need a new milker, right?"

I nodded.

"Why not raise your own, Dad? Why not clear out five acres of the forest near the river and raise your own? Livestock will have access to the runoff brook and pond and..."

"That is very ambitious of you to think of that," I said. "Wish I was that ambitious. Let's get you through Active Service first. Then you can come back and get into farming."

Brad thought it over then murmured, "Sky will love seeing calves born."

I rolled my eyes. "Here we go with Sky again."

He turned beet red. Then his wide, deep blue eyes soft-soaped me. "Come on, Dad."

Oh, yeah, my son could still pull my strings. And of course, I wanted to please my long-lost daughter. On the other hand, I was not going to give in all that easily. I feigned a grumble. "I'm too old and much too lazy, and now I have two offspring, neither of which carries my name and..."

"I never did understand why my last name didn't change to yours when you adopted me," he said.

"Because at the time, you were vehemently opposed to it," I said.

"I can't imagine why, Dad. Gosh, what an annoying kid I was. How did you ever put up with me?"

"You were a brave young soul. You went through so much pain and sorrow that all I wanted to do was to take all your troubles away. From the start, you were the kind of boy I always wanted for a son. I wanted to take you home and love you. I hated to see you cry. I worried that changing your name was just going to cause you more pain."

Brad interlaced his fingers in front of his mouth, obviously reliving painfully memories. He looked away for a moment then back at me. He reached for my hand. "I want to be Brad Brendan."

Choking back a tear, I gave a decisive nod.

"But won't that cause a lot of problems with the Army?" he asked.

"It shouldn't," I said. "Women in the military get married and change their names all the time. Some people just don't like their names, so they change them legally."

"Let's get Aunt Lisa on it, Dad."

"Knowing her, it'll get done before you leave."

CHAPTER SIXTEEN

At breakfast the next morning, Brad asked Lisa to do whatever was needed to make the name change. Everyone clapped as if a great staged artistry had just been performed. I glanced at Sky. What's she thinking? Did she want her name changed, too? I cast that notion aside. It's too soon after Marie's death to pursue that.

Worried about the lingering rain, most of us headed off to nine o'clock Mass. Much to my delight, Sky was a practicing Catholic. Brad had become one during counseling sessions with Father Francis, and now, even away from home, he still maintained his religion.

It was well known that Dolly was a person who didn't go about making meals haphazardly. Endless plans were made, lists handed out to the *volunteers* she roped in. Though new to the fold, Sky wasn't excused from helping out. Truth be known, that's exactly what Sky wanted.

"Come on, let's hop-to!" Dolly snapped, slapping her hands together. "There's work to be done! Let's go! Let's go!"

So after changing out of Sunday-best into casual, I set up tables for the kiddies in the sunroom and a full size table to seat more than a dozen adults. Thankfully, rain had turned into mist. Now if the sun would only come out.

"Brad and Sky are too grown up to sit with the kids," I said. "We're going to have to consider Brad and Sky adults and…"

Dolly gawked at me, hands on hips. "No kidding, Dick Tracy."

I rolled my eyes. "There'll still be a mess of kids in this sunroom."

"Don't count baby Donald," Dolly said. "His mother will be holding him."

"No kidding, Dick Tracy," I jabbed.

Dolly huffed, turned on a dime, and marched off to the kitchen.

I chuckled then went out to the workshop to get sawhorses and boards for the tabletops. The sun looked like it was trying to come out.

As I set up the folding chairs Lisa rented, I considered myself lucky doing these simple jobs. I wouldn't have wanted to cook. Dolly claimed I never could cook a decent meal. Besides, she wouldn't let me anyway.

Heather drove her van onto the grass on the other side of the driveway opposite the back door. Leo got out of the front passenger seat and slid open the rear door. He unhooked the infant carrier then took it out, never disturbing the sleeping Donald. Jill, Judy, Chris, and Barry barreled out the other side of the van, yelping, "Where's Sky?"

I pointed at my daughter exiting the house. Shielding her eyes from the sun, she acted like the lady of the manor, which I thought was rather nice.

The four children raced to her and nearly knocked her down. "Are you really our cousin?"

Stunned momentarily, she then gathered herself together and asked, "Is Frank really your Uncle?"

"Yup!"

She giggled. "Okay. So your Uncle Frank is your Dad's brother, right?"

"Yup!"

She nodded decisively. "Okay! Since Frank is my Dad; that makes you my cousins!"

"Cool!" they exclaimed. For the rest of the day, they hounded her. All the kids seemed to want a piece of her. I felt like I should help her get away from them, but then she'd survive. She's young and healthy. But what if she thinks having so many cousins wasn't as great as she once thought? On the other hand, it was plain as the nose on my face that she adored five-year-old Barry and baby Donald. I grunted. "I better mind my own business."

Susie and Jerry arrived with Janet and Cameron. Janet was the same age as Jill and Judy, the three hung out all the time, but Janet wasn't as forward as the twins. Janet spoke timidly and that was okay with Sky who noticed a larger group arriving. It was her Uncle John, Uncle Joey and their wives Linda and Carla - and six more children: Paul, Jack, Dan, Andrew, Kate and Karen.

Even Father Francis showed up again!

Later, Sky told me, "It blew my mind that there were so many people so important to me! Everybody was talking all at once! What a clamor! A couple times, I felt like running up to my room and hiding, but I just couldn't, because I was really looking forward to this get-together and I knew in a blink of an eye it will all be over and done with. So I kicked myself in the pants; what's the matter with you, Sky? And instead of running away, I helped Dolly with the food. Then I took Dan and Karen for a walk, I figured I could handle a three-year-old boy and a four-year-old girl. But Brad was in his glory, wasn't he? He ate up all the commotion."

"I have all the confidence in the world that in time, you will grow to love it, just the way Brad did when I took him in," I said. "Guess I never shy away from family commotion, because I was born into it."

Earlier, though, I did notice Father Francis appearing to be overwhelmed. I stepped over to him and shouted above the din, "I set a place for you on the veranda."

He laughed that boisterous laugh of his and said, "No, no, I can't stay. I just wanted to drop in for a moment after seeing so many of you at Mass this morning." He tipped his cap. "I'll be on my way, now."

The food was incredible, and I was incredibly starved! The kids took their plates outside. My efforts in the sunroom turned out for naught. Then again, those kids had a lot of energy to get rid of.

Lisa took over little Dan and Karen who sorely needed naps. Sky helped the rest of the women with the clean-up, while John, Leo, and I broke down tables and chairs in the sunroom. As we headed out to the workshop with sawhorses and boards, Brad was rounding up the children. "Who wants a tour of the barn?"

Squeals of delight filled the air.

I trailed them into the barn where Brad and a couple of hands answered questions about the cows, the milking process, and the stink. Several children climbed the ladder and disappeared into the hayloft. Moments later, a scream sent Brad charging up the ladder. I looked up from the bottom and hollered, "What's going up there?"

"A rat!" the twins squawked in unison.

Chris and Andy roared with laughter. "It's only a little tiny mouse!"

The twins scurried down the ladder. "Your cats sure aren't doing their jobs, Uncle Frank."

"I don't have any cats," I said.

"What? No cats?" Jill asked. "All farms have cats!"

I jounced my hands out to my sides and shrugged.

Judy jabbed me in the ribs. "We got loads of cats and kittens over our place, Uncle Frank. You better drop over tomorrow and help yourself."

"But I..."

Brad cut me off. "Good idea! Sky and I will be there first thing in the morning."

By sunset, most guests had left and I was standing on the back stoop, watching Brad and Sky set off for a walk. Brad wanted to check the forest and pond for future reference. I heard him say, "Sure wish we had horses."

"Maybe when you're done with the Army," Sky said.

His voice faded in the shadows, "Dad and I were thinking along the very same lines."

Gee, I thought he only wanted milkers.

CHAPTER SEVENTEEN

"**H**ave you ever ridden a horse?" I asked Sky the next morning at breakfast.

Her mouth was chocked full of cereal, so she shook her head. She chewed quickly then swallowed. "No, my Dad...my other Dad...was in the Army and horses weren't anywhere near the places he was stationed."

"Uncle Leo has horses," Brad said.

"Maybe we can learn to ride his ride horses before you go off to Active Duty," Sky said.

"Those are work horses," I said. "I believe they can't be ridden."

Disappointment sheeted Sky's face.

"Listen, I'll pick you up after school," Brad said, "and then we'll stop by Uncle Leo's and find out for sure. We have to stop there for the cats anyway."

Her face lit up. "Good thing spring vacation starts at school, next week. We'll have the whole week to learn how to ride."

I glanced at the kitchen clock. "You two better get going or else Sky's going to be late for school her first day."

Sky raced out the door, Brad right behind. "I'll be right back, Dad," he said. "Wait for me to do the chores." Ever since Brad was eleven, he enjoyed doing farm chores. By the time he got back, the hands had finished milking and were letting the cows out to pasture. "I'll be able to get to chores earlier next week," he promised," since I won't have to take Sky to school." He donned waterproof gear over his jeans and tee shirt then hosed down the barn. "Sky says she didn't mind the smell. She's just like me; I hated it at first; it made me gag. Now, it doesn't bother either one of us. Guess we were born to this life." He swept manure through the gullies, which ended up in the septic tank.

That afternoon, Brad drove the old Buick to Oakridge High School, picked up Sky, and headed off to Leo's Farm, the name of the farm. They pulled up to the house first and said hello to Heather who was busy with baby Donald. Then they went to the field where Jill, Judy, Chris and Barry were helping Leo and three other men setting up tomato plant cages. "Look at you guys go!" Brad said.

Leo rolled his eyes. "Not easy training these kids of mine. But at their age, I suppose they're coming along okay."

The twins, being the oldest figured they were the boss. Jill was a natural at it, but Judy got flustered. So Leo interceded, "Judy, take Brad and Sky to barn and track down those kittens."

Sky was smitten with a tri-colored mama cat and her three kittens, especially the orange tiger kitten. The other two were tri-colored like the mama, money cats, as old wives called them.

"You have to take Mama Cat even though the kittens are weaned, because the kittens don't know how to hunt mice yet," Judy said. "And you better get them fixed or you'll get lots of kittens like we do. We have much too many cats."

The box Sky and Brad brought proved useless. Mama Cat kept picking up her brood by the scruffs of their necks and trying to relocate them. So Judy hunted down an old rabbit cage that did the job. But now, Mama Cat didn't want Papa Cat in the rabbit cage with her babies. "You better come back later and get him," Judy said. With Mama Cat and kittens safely caged in the backseat of the old Buick, Brad and Sky headed to the field again to talk to Leo.

"So your Dad told me you were interested in enlarging the farm and raising cattle," Leo said.

Brad winked at Sky. "I'm thinking about horses, too. But that's a ways off. In the meantime, Sky and I want to learn to ride, so how about teaching us to ride yours?"

Leo shook his head. "Mine are work horses; never ridden. They'd go hog-wild if you tried. I suggest you go to Harry's Riding Ranch over in Swain and get lessons from someone who knows what he's doing."

"Thanks, Uncle Leo," Brad said. "Come on, Sky, let's take Mama Cat and her babies home.

After, we'll go pick up supplies for them at This And That. Kind of reminds me of the day I brought Buddy home for the first time. We'll pick up Papa Cat on the way home. Looks like we have to wait until tomorrow to go over to Swain and check out Harry's horses."

Sky wanted the orange tiger for a pet, so when she and Brad got home, she took it to her room. She named it, Light. Brad set Mama Cat and her two other kittens loose in the barn.

The next afternoon, Brad and Sky drove out to Harry's Riding Ranch. Harry took them into the stable to meet the horses. "They're so big," she said. "Scary thinking of getting up on top of one."

"We don't have to do this," Brad said.

"Oh, but I really want to, Brad."

Harry gave them the price of riding lessons and arranged for lessons three days a week. Brad was so thrilled he paid Harry up front for eleven lessons.

CHAPTER EIGHTEEN

When Brad and Sky told me about their plans to learn to ride, I was afraid. What if one - or both - fell and got hurt? "Calm down, Dad," Brad said. "We're taking lessons. We'll be fine."

But I went with them for the first lesson - just to be on the safe side.

Harry had the horses in the paddock and ready to go. He introduced the three of us to the horses. "Here, feed them these carrots and they'll be your best friends for life."

Brad's horse, Thor, was big and black with a white ring around his throat. Sky's horse, Cocoa, was somewhat smaller, chocolate brown with a white moon shape on her forehead.

After fifteen minutes of patting their snouts, giving them carrots, and talking to them, I stepped back and let Brad and Sky take the reins in their hands. As they walked the horses around the paddock, Harry said, "You two are naturals." He stepped over to a set of wooden steps. "Bring your horses over here. You need these steps to get on them for the first few times. Here you go, Brad, I want you to do three things: put your left foot in the stirrup; put your hand on the front piece of the saddle; and throw your right leg over the other side."

Brad performed the task flawlessly.

"Your turn Sky," Harry said.

She walked Cocoa over to the steps. She eyed the saddle, so high up, and then down at the steps. She pursed her lips. Next thing I knew, there she was, way up in that saddle.

"When you want to go forward," Harry said, "position your leg against the horse like this and apply a little pressure." He took the double rein in his hand and arranged it between his fingers. "To stop or go slower, apply a little pressure like this." He demonstrated a slight tightening of the reins. "You need to direct the horses, not only with the reins, but also with your knees. By pressing your left knee on your horse, you go right; your right knee to go left. Okay now, move around the paddock and get used to the motion of the horse. Hold your body straight, that way you won't be apt to lose your balance or be thrown off. I suggest you don't wear short pants or you'll end up with chafed and very sore skin." Harry and I watched them for several moments then he said, "So what do you say? You think you're going to like horseback riding?"

Sky grinned. "Yes! I love it!"

Brad chuckled. "I'm looking forward to riding through fields and forests and small ponds."

Harry glanced at his watch. "Lessons are an hour and a half each, so you have fifteen minutes left, today. Circle the paddock and use up the rest of the time. Today, I will take care of your horses; however, your next lesson includes the proper care of horses, so you'll be responsible for that at the end of each lesson."

"Sky and I need to know how to keep horses clean and healthy," Brad said.

Sky nodded. "Yup! Someday, we are going to own horses."

On the way home, I sat in the back seat of the old Buick, listening to Brad and Sky chatter on and on about their new endeavor. Brad seemed fascinated by Sky: her smiles; her flushed face. I could just read his mind: It won't be long before he planned to kiss those enchanting lips of hers. I could tell they were getting real close - and that pleased me - *and* scared me.

Later that night, Brad went on and on about having horses and building barns. I told him again, "We'll consider all that when you're done with Active Duty." I gave him a sidelong look. "I see you're sweet on Sky, but let me warn you, my son, I have never hit you, but if Sky ever becomes pregnant because of your carelessness, I'll beat the hell out of you. That's a guarantee."

He gawked at me. "Wow, Dad, talk about straight-talk."

I hooked my chin. "That's what father's do."

"Look, Dad, Sky is precious to me, too; and I promise you, I will treat her with all the respect she is due. You will never have to beat the hell out of me."

Just then Sky walked in. "I fed and watered the barn cats."

I spoke up, "Those cats won't catch one single mouse if you keep feeding them like that."

She waved me off. "I went online and found out it's truly necessary to feed barn cats, since there might not be enough mice in the barn to keep them well. And cats *do* need water."

Brad and I exchanged twinkles of the eyes.

"While I was patting ol' Bossy..."

"You were patting the cows again?" Brad asked, faking astonishment.

She nodded.

"You don't pat cows," he said.

She gave him a scornful huff. "Of course you do, silly. Anyways, while I was doing that, Poppy came in; and we got to talking about future plans and riding lessons. Poppy thinks your idea is fantastic; and he's going to convince Frank to look kindly on it."

"Let's not go getting ahead of ourselves," I said, watching Sky scoot up the stairs.

A downcast look swept over Brad. "It's not going to happen, huh, Dad?"

"I didn't say that," I said.

A short time later, we were in the kitchen, chatting with Dolly and Nanny. Sky was standing at the window, cuddling Light. "Lisa's coming."

Dolly jumped to her feet, "Good heavens, I have to get food on the table!"

Our hearts skipped beats, for we knew what Lisa was going to say. Before she could even shut off the engine, Brad was opening her car door. "Did you do it, Aunt Lisa?"

"Of course! It's done and over with. You are now officially Brad Brendon. Next thing is to let the Army know and have the government change your name and send you a new Social Security card. I have the papers right here with addressed envelopes of where to send information."

Brad strutted into the kitchen, proud as a peacock. His eyes skimmed us then focused on me. His hands swept his body head toe. "I would like to introduce to you me, Brad Louis Brendan."

I shook his hand and slapped him on the back. "How do you do, Brad Brendan?"

As Nanny, Poppy, Lisa, and Dolly hugged and congratulated him, an odd look swept over Sky.

"What's the matter?" Brad asked.

She looked me straight in the eye. "I suppose you think I should change my name."

I was temporarily tongue-tied.

"Well, I don't feel comfortable doing that," she said. "Because the man whose last name was

Farmer was my father for a very long time. He was a good father - and a good man - and a hero who died for our country. My mother, who just died, was proud of him. And she loved him. And I feel it would be dishonoring him - and dishonoring her - to change my name."

I cleared my throat. "I never expected you to feel otherwise. I'm proud of you for honoring your loved ones, those who took care of you so well and caused you to be the wonderful person you are." I took a deep breath and smiled. "One way or the other, Sky Farmer, I am proud to have you and Brad Brendon as my children."

Sky beamed with pleasure. She hugged me. Then she hugged Brad, saying, "Congratulations, Brad Brendan.

CHAPTER NINETEEN

Two days later, Brad and Sky were back at Harry's Riding Ranch. Later, when they got home, they didn't miss one iota of detail:

"We tried to mount the horses without the stairs, unsuccessfully," Sky said. "'That's okay,' Harry told us. 'We'll work on that tomorrow.'"

"After riding around the paddock for an hour, we got into the care of horses," Brad said. "Harry demonstrated while talking. 'Let's start with the basics. This is called an outback saddle, which is much lighter on the horse than other saddles. This in the front is a handhold. Most horses trot or jog a lot, so the outback saddle is easier to post on. Posting is a two beat movement the rider does. It's up on one beat and down on the two beat and timed to the horse's trot so as not to be bouncing all over the back of the horse.

"'The front piece of the saddle is the pommel and the back is the cantle. When sliding up the stirrups, you tuck the straps through the stirrup iron to secure it, so it doesn't fall down.

"'To remove the bridle, unbuckle the cheek strap before lifting the crown gently over the ears. Be sure when you lower the bridle that you take the bit out of the horse's mouth, carefully; don't chunk it against its teeth.

"'Over here is the tack room where we store all the gear that you just removed.

"'The best way to work on a horse, whether washing it completely or just sponging it off, is to cross tie it. The horse must have a halter on and you attach two lead ropes to the halter. Some people will ground tie horses, but this is very unusual and there is no control if the horse gets spooked while you are working on it.

"'Here is the water hose to rinse the horse. Then you scrape off the excess water. Once the coat is dry, use this brush to shine up the coat. Always brush in the direction the hair grows.

"'It may seem like a lot of work, but it really isn't, plus it is so important to the wellbeing of the horse, which is an expensive animal, so you must not be careless with his treatment.

"'Cleaning a horse is more involved if you have been out for a long time. I'll be happy to explain that to you at another time if you wish.'"

"Brad and I took a lot of pleasure brushing down Thor and Cocoa," Sky said. "While doing so, we jabbered on and on to the horses."

"No kidding," I said wryly.

Brad let Sky drive to Oakridge, so she could get used to the car and get her Oklahoma driver's license at the Department of Motor Vehicles. Luckily, all she had to do was have her picture taken with her new address on it. No test! Yay!

After that, they stopped to see Lisa at work then went to lunch with her. Lisa told Sky to drop in after school anytime. Sky promised to do so, on days she didn't have riding lessons. That's when Lisa said, "Someday, I'm going to learn how to ride."

On the way home, Brad told Sky, "Next week, you take the car to school, and on afternoons we have riding lessons, I'll meet you at Harry's.

"I can't take the car, Brad. You need it."

"No, I don't. I can get all over town on my bike."

"That's too hard," Sky protested.

"No, it's not, Sky. I used to do it all the time. I'll enjoy it. Honest."

At the beginning of the next lesson, they succeeded in mounting their horses without stairs. Talk about proud - I didn't hear the end of it for days.

Riding came easier and really enjoyable. Harry allowed them onto the racetrack where they went a lot faster than in the paddock area. They claimed it was so invigorating, and Harry ended up calling them in to groom their horses. They got to love the animals so much that they hated to leave them. Both dreamed of the day when they owned a barn filled with horses that they could ride whenever they wanted.

The next week, Sky went back to school and Bran spent mornings, working in the dairy. Their riding lessons continued after school.

CHAPTER TWENTY

The farewell dinner for Nanny and Poppy was held on Sunday. They were leaving for Texas bright and early Monday morning. The weather was fantastic, so a barbeque was served outside and the kids ran at will. Sky handled the commotion better than the last get-together. In fact, she enjoyed it immensely. She even made friends with the twins and came to realize how clever they were.

"How come you walk around hugging your cat like that?" Jill asked.

"Her name is Light," Sky said. "She's my pet and I enjoy loving her like this."

"Wow," Judy said. "We don't never treat animals like they was pets."

"I used to be like that," Brad said, coming up behind the three. They turned to him as he added, "But since I met Sky, I've changed. I even found out I love horses more than I thought I did." As he fingered her shoulder-length curls, I watched from afar. I sensed this young couple's hopes: Someday to give their love to one another. She gazed at him, so tall, wiry, and blond, as if he were a Viking of old. He didn't seem to be missing the way she was gazing at him either. Now he was drowning in her green eyes. Were they about to kiss one another? He's going to lose control someday, and I was going to have to take a strap to him. Suddenly, I felt like a peeping Tom. I ran my hand through my hair. I had to stop thinking such thoughts. I walked away, lying to myself about having to check on the barn cats. I found them thriving.

Though Brad and Sky spent much of the next three weeks together, she did enjoy school. She made friends with Mary O'Brien and Billie Gibbs. They lived in Middle and had cars. However, the three carpooled to save on gas, except on days Sky had horseback riding. They ate in the lunchroom together and got together often on weekends. Billie's family had horses, so Sky was offered free use of their horses. "I can't impose on your family that way," Sky said.

"You'll be doing us a favor," Billie said. "My brother moved to LA, so our horses, which he used to ride, really need exercise."

Time passed too quickly, and Brad was going off to Fort Hood, Texas, for nine months of training before being deployed to Afghanistan. He and Sky did go to the barn. They did get that kiss they both had been longing for. They did not let it progress any further. I know because Brad told me so. They didn't dare let that kiss go any further. Yes, it would have been so easy to let it get out of hand. Only the cows and the cats would have seen...

Sky and I drove Brad to the airport on Saturday. We were so sad to see him go; and he was sad to go.

Her lips trembled as she made every effort to be brave, to hold back the tears. Mine trembled, too.

The three of us were dreading this day - and yet, here it was. I wished I could stop it. The time, I mean. Oh, why did I ever sign that ROTC form? Now all I had to look forward to was him coming home in nine months for five measly days before he goes on Active Duty - to Afghanistan, no less. I know: on rare occasions he would call; and he planned to e-mail often. Thank God for e-mails, at least they are easy to get out.

It was a silent ride home.

CHAPTER TWENTY-ONE

The town gala, held yearly on May 30th, was the first for Sky. Mary and Billie had been going since the year 2000, when they were seven years old. They raved about it. Sky was surprised to learn it had originally been held on my farm to welcome Brad into Middle. Now it took place on a field in the center of town. There was always plenty of food. Charles Woodward still furnished a pig and roasted it, too. Four families furnished hamburgers while four other families furnished chicken.

Many former Middle citizens, including Lisa, returned for the gala and brought donations. This year, Mom and Dad didn't come, since they had just returned to Texas.

As always the gala was a huge success, which made Sky feel more and more like Middle was home. She really perked up when her friends talked about organizing a parade next year. "We could dress up in fancy duds and ride our horses in the parade," Billie said.

Sky had been going to Billie's and riding Ginger, so named because of its color. Sky had gotten very attached to the sweet horse. Billie usually rode a gray horse called Dusty.

Billie turned to Mary. "You need to learn how to ride, so you can ride in the parade with us. Sky and I will teach you. My horse named Mazie is gentle as a lamb."

The color drained from Mary's face. "I-I guess so."

Sky wondered: Was Mary truly interested? Or was Mary afraid of horses?

That night Sky emailed Brad about the wonderful time she had at the gala and about the parade plans for next year. She told him about Billie's offer to teach Mary how to ride and how scared Mary looked.

Brad replied: Not a good idea to press Mary. She might do it just to please everyone, but her fear might get her hurt.

Sky emailed back: Never thought about that. I'll tell Billie what you said tomorrow.

Nevertheless, Billie was not to be swayed. "Mary will love riding Mazie," she insisted, while leading Mazie out of the stall.

Mary stayed at a distance.

After saddling Mazie, Billie beckoned, "Get over here, Mary!"

"Wait," Sky said. "Harry had Brad and me make friends with our horses first. That's what Mary should do."

Billie huffed and puffed, but in the end, gave in. "Here, Mary, give this carrot to Mazie."

Mary backed away, acting as if Billie was terrorizing her. "I-I can't."

"What do you mean, 'You can't'?" Billie snapped.

"I-I know you won't...want to be my friends anymore, but...I just can't do this. Horses are too big and scary."

"You don't have to do this to be my friend," Sky said. "That's ridiculous. We're friends because I like you, and that's that."

Billie was not as understanding. "At least Mary could *try* to like horses."

Sky glared at Billie. "If Mary is afraid of horses, she can do something else in the parade."

That night Sky told me what went down that afternoon. "You're right not to insist on Mary learning to ride. When she was seven years old, she saw her father thrown off a horse. He was in a coma for three months before he died. After that kind of trauma at such a young age, it's understandable that Mary has a longstanding fear of horses."

Sky called Billie and explained Mary's fear. "We are not to pressure Mary to make friends with horses. I am keeping her as a friend. I hope you do, too."

In her nightly email to Brad, Sky let him know how right he was about not forcing Mary to interact with horses, telling him about Mary's father. As she typed, her cat Light kneaded her arm, looking for attention. Buddy was snoozing against her leg, his head braced against her knee. The two pets got along splendidly. Light was brave enough to bat Buddy with a paw and he liked it. Often, they licked each other clean then fell asleep together.

The cell phone rang. Sky flipped it open without checking the caller ID. She just assumed it was either Billie or Mary.

"Miss me, sweetheart?"

"Brad!" Sky exclaimed. "Oh boy, do I! Gosh! It's great hearing your voice! Hold on while I put the phone on speaker. I want Buddy to hear your voice. He's here with Light on my bed. You won't believe how awesome they get along."

"Hey, Buddy boy," Brad said. "Do you miss me, too?"

Buddy pushed his nose up to the phone.

"He's looking for you, Brad. His tail is wagging so hard, his entire backside is wobbling. He looks like he's smiling."

Sky and Brad talked for about one hour. I would have liked to talk to him, too, but I was at a Grange meeting at the time. When I got home, Sky told me about his call.

As it turned out, Mary never did learn to ride. More often than not, Sky invited Mary and Billie to our house or to go on shopping trips. Mary was quite relieved to keep Sky and Billie as friends without having to be around too many horses.

Summer vacation began. Even though I expected Sky to do a few chores in the dairy every day, I urged her to learn more about the business end of things. I wanted her and Brad to take over the farm that my grandfather started - especially now that Howie planned to retire when winter came. Plus he shouldn't be working so hard during the heat of summer. Sky was completely on-board, so Howie took on the job of teaching her. I felt relieved, since the seventy-five-year-old had been looking pretty frail of late.

So my other two hands, Ron and Craig, and I worked the farm. But who was going to take over Howie's job? Ron? Craig? Which reminded me, I had to ask them when they wanted to take their two-week paid vacations.

One way or the other, I didn't want Sky working her entire summer vacation, so I posted a schedule on the barn bulletin board, giving her plenty of free time to be with her friends. Luckily, Ron and Craig chose winter vacations.

Sky took to the business like a real Brendan. Every time Brad called, I heard her chattering on and on about the work as if it was fun. That's when I decided to convert a section of the barn into stables and buy two horses.

CHAPTER TWENTY-TWO

Just as life usually goes, changes happen. Billie found a boyfriend. He was a friend of her cousin. He lived in Oakridge and was attending a nearby college, so he still lived at home. It didn't take Sky and Mary long to realize that they wouldn't be seeing much of Billie.

Billie's father assured Sky that she was always welcome to ride the horses. Because evenings were light until after 8 o'clock, she went every Wednesday and Friday after supper. She figured that her days would be full with working the business and on her days off, she wanted to spend with Mary.

One day, Mary and Sky dropped in to see Mary's mother, Helen O'Brien, who worked at Abby's This And That. Mrs. O'Brien was an attractive woman with dark wavy hair and deep blue eyes. Sky thought Mrs. O'Brien was a wonderful mother, like hers had been.

"So nice of you two to drop by," Mrs. O'Brien said. She patted Sky's arm. "Your friendship has made Mary a new person."

After a while, a customer came in, so Mary and Sky left and went next door to Louie's Pizza and Sub Shop. "How wonderful to see you two!" Mary's maternal grandmother, Julia Beam, exclaimed. While serving them pizza, she said, "So you're Frank Brendan's daughter. You know, I can still remember when the Brendan family arrived. Such a nice family. The whole town got interested in them. Wow, did the single girls in these parts set their sights on your father! I am surprised he stayed single."

"I've been wondering that same thing," Sky said. That's when she got the idea to set me up with Mrs. O'Brien. On the way home she told Mary about it; and of course, Mary was gung-ho. Well, I won't get into their plans, as none of their ideas worked out. You see Mary's mother had a boyfriend - and it wasn't me.

After lunch, Mary took Sky to her house, which was a small cottage at the edge of town. Mary let her and Sky in with her key. The attractive cottage resembled the home Sky grew up in, and she felt very much at ease there. So while Mary poured two glasses of iced tea, Sky leafed through a photo album that was on the coffee table. Spotting a picture of a very handsome young man, she asked, "Who's this?"

"My brother," Mary said, setting the glasses on the coffee table next to the album. "Bobby is twenty-five, eight years older than me."

"I love his hair," Sky said, admiring the long, shiny, jet black waves.

Mary heaved a sigh. "He looks like my Dad. Bobby was fifteen-years-old when Dad died. He didn't handle it good at all. He just went crazy."

"I know how that feels," Sky said.

"He got in touch with us, just last week," Mary said. "He's been gone an awful long time."

"Is he coming home?"

"Supposed to be. In a couple of days. Hope he does."

"You must be so looking forward to seeing him."

Mary nodded. "Mom pushed Bobby real hard to graduate, and he barely did. Then he joined the Marines. It was real tough for all of us. But he made a first grade Marine."

"So now he's getting out and coming home," Sky said.

Mary nodded again. "He worked on all kinds of vehicles in the Marines. Mom says he's hoping to land a job as a mechanic here."

Bobby O'Brien arrived home just like he said he would. He was taller than I had known him to be, six-feet-four now, and his jet black hair was cut short, so short he looked bald. He used money he saved while in the Marines to put an offer in on an old garage that had gas tanks. An elderly man, who ran the place for over fifty years, had it up for sale for quite some time, so he was quite content to scoop up Bobby's first offer.

Bobby O'Brien was a soft-spoken, kind young man, so he got along just fine with townsfolk. Sky became friendly with him, since Mary went often to see him at the garage, often bringing lunch. Mary was elated to have her brother back. He lived with her and their mother; although, he planned to get an apartment of his own. Sky was around him so much I wondered if she was sweet on him. I didn't approve of them as a couple; Bobby was too old for her.

Sky still went horseback riding. I chastised myself for not buying a horse for her by now; and for not getting around to building the said horse a stall yet. "I'll get right on that. It'll be a good way to keep Sky home. I could give her more work in the barn. Oh boy, kids are a lot of trouble."

CHAPTER TWENTY-THREE

The phone rang just as I got in from the barn before supper. Dolly was in the kitchen, but since I was beside the phone, I took it. It was Brad. I was ecstatic! I hadn't talked to him in a long time! We talked forty-five minutes. We guzzled each others' news like cool drinks of water. When Sky walked in, I said, "Want to talk to Brad?"

"You bet I do!"

They talked another hour.

Dolly whispered in my ear, "I guess I don't get to talk to our boy this time."

I tapped Sky on the shoulder. "How about giving Dolly a couple minutes?"

Dolly didn't talk long, but it was apparent that she was in her glory talking to him. She reluctantly hung up.

"Is it all right if I invite Mary and her mother and grandmother for Sunday dinner?" Sky asked at the supper table Thursday night.

"Bobby, too?" I spouted, my mouth full of mashed potatoes.

Sky gave me the evil eye.

"I planned to take this Sunday off," Dolly said.

"That's okay," Sky said. "I'll do the cooking."

"Do you think you're a good enough cook to not poison them?" I joked while slicing off a piece of roast chicken.

Again the evil eye. "I can read a cookbook."

I shrugged. "Good enough. I'll lend a hand."

She stuck out her chin. "I can handle it all by myself."

Again I shrugged. "All you have to do is ask."

On Sunday, Mary, her mother, Helen O'Brien, and her grandmother, Julia Beam, arrived at 11 a.m. Oh, and let's not forget Bobby. He came later - in his brand new car.

Sky baked a giant lasagna and southern style rolls from the dairy section. She made chocolate cream pie with a graham cracker crust for dessert. Everything turned out splendid; and she blushed from all the compliments.

Somehow, this inept father managed to set the table and pour guests their preferred drinks.

Helen O'Brien was a pretty middle aged woman. Perhaps I should take an interest in her. Sky would like that. I glanced at my daughter. Well, will you look at the way she's shining up to that Bobby? Like he's the best thing since sliced bread. I gritted my teeth. Yeah, that got my goat.

Summer flew by, and Sky was using most of it, working in the barn. Other times, she drove to Leo's farm and spent time with her cousins, bringing home fresh vegetables every time. Now and then, she stopped off to see John at his office or went to see Abby or stopped by the vet clinic to see Joey and help with the animals. She also managed to squeeze in visits to Aunt Susie and others. What a busy little lady. I was glad she didn't have much time to spend with Bobby. Sadly, Mary found a new girlfriend, but that didn't appear to bother Sky much.

I finally got around to building the stable. When I asked Sky if she wanted to go with me on an eighty-mile trip to check out some horses, of course she said, "Yes."

At the Wellington Ranch, I told the owner, "I want two horses no more than three years old."

He took us to a field where half a dozen horses were jousting about. "They look kind of frisky," I said. "They might be hard to ride."

"Young healthy horses are frisky," the owner said. "You should look for friskiness."

"They look wonderful," Sky said. "I like the chocolate brown one with the white face! And the one over there, the black one with white spots, that's Brad's horse!"

I was a bit leery. "Let's take a look at them up close."

"Sure thing," the owner said. He handed us some carrots.

I fed the black horse. Sky fed the brown one. Up close, we fell in love with those two horses. "Sold," I said.

On the way home, Sky didn't let me get in a single word. "The brown horse is mine. Her name is Misty. The black horse is Brad's. We have to take a picture of him and send it to Brad, so he can name him."

On Tuesday, I don't know who was more excited when that horse trailer came rambling down the road. By then, Sky had convinced me that she could teach me how to ride; and I was excited about that.

We had gone on line to find out what to feed young horses and how often. Then we went to the grain store to buy feed, saddles, riding clothes, you name it. We got everything we thought we needed and more.

Brad named his horse Sarge. Talk about thrilled. He could hardly wait to get home and ride him. When I told him Sky was going to teach me to ride, he emailed: Wish I could see that!!!

His levity gave me second thoughts. Was I really going to ride a horse? At my age? The next day, I had my first lesson. I surprised myself. I had no problems getting on Sarge. Being on top of a horse was a heady and exhilarating feeling. And I wasn't sore afterwards.

Misty and Sarge made surprisingly nice pets. They enjoyed being ridden and pampered.

One day, Sky and I took a ride through the woods. "It's been a long time since I've been out this trail. It leads to the pond where my family used to go on hot days to take a swim."

When we got to the pond, Sky said, "What a lovely spot. So serene. Won't it be nice when Brad gets here and he and I ride out here?"

"What am I chopped liver?" I asked.

"No, Dad, but you're Dad. A really great Dad, but you're just Dad."

I was satisfied with being *just Dad*.

Sky began her senior year. Howie retired and went to Texas to live in the same senior park where Mom and Dad lived. Sky pitched in, filling the gap Howie left. The first of December, a heavy snowstorm hit. School got called off for two days. The next week, the weather warmed up, so most of the snow melted.

On January 8th, Sky and I picked up Brad at the airport. Surprise plastered her face. "Wow, Brad! You're all muscles!"

There was no sign of the boy I had known. He was all man. Although he was still boy enough to give us huge hugs. Funny how he kissed Sky on her lips.

After picking up his duffle bag, we headed home where Dolly was creating a feast. I was glad I had broken down and put up the stable and purchased two fine horses. Brad checked all of it out right away. "Thanks Dad," he said, patting Sarge. "I really appreciate this. Wish I could spend more than only for a few days here. Sky will love all this though."

"I've been riding," I said. "Sky is a great teacher."

Dolly hollered from the porch, "Hey, you guys. Get in here and wash up. Supper is ready."

Brad gave Dolly a bear hug before washing up. She slapped him playfully on the chest, saying, "Oh, you silly boy!"

Conversation at the table went full blast. Dolly wanted to know when Brad had to leave and where he was going.

"I'm off to Afghanistan," he said.

Dolly put her napkin to her mouth, which was an inadequate attempt to hide her horror.

"Now don't you guys assume I'll be in the thick of things, because it's more likely I won't. Anyhow, the training I went through was unbelievable, so I know I am a good and clever soldier. I'll get through this in one piece. Now, for the next week, I intend to enjoy being home, especially since Dad furnished Sky and me horses. Hey Dolly, I've been meaning to ask you: Have you gotten any news from your grandson Jason? I lost touch with him when we went on Active Duty."

Dolly sighed. "Sue told me he's doing fine. Did you know he's going to become a pilot and plans to make it his life's work?"

"How about that! Good for him! Where is he? You have to give me his email address."

"I know he'd love to hear from you."

After supper Brad and Sky did the cleanup then headed out to saddle the horses. "Their laughter makes me smile," I said.

"Am I the only one who is scared out of my mind?" Dolly asked, stepping over to the window. "That place he's heading is awful. Our boys are getting killed over there. Or do you have to be young and foolish not to realize that?"

I stepped over to the window and took hold of her hand."You and I have done a lot of living and can see the awful possibilities. Believe me when I say, I'm frightened for my son." We soon spotted Brad and Sky riding out of the stable. "They're headed to the pond," I said.

"But it's frozen over," Dolly said.

I sighed. "We have to let them enjoy their time together."

CHAPTER TWENTY-FOUR

The sun was setting on the last day of Brad's leave. Watching him and Sky ride off into the forest, I imagined the iced-over pond, a plaid horse blanket spread upon the frozen grass. She would probably ask him if he was afraid to go. Knowing Brad like I do, he would tell a white lie, "Not at all."

My imagination ran wild. Why? Because long, long ago, I had been in a similar situation - with Sky's mother...

He stared at her, a flush of warmth rose within, strengthening, thickening, until he realized what it was. He was aroused. His body yearned to give her what she wanted. He longed to hold her, to love her, to fill her with his seed. The reaction was so barbaric and inappropriate that it mortified him. He felt her gaze.

Their desires flared high and wild. Her delicate fingers caressed his cheeks, his jaw, scraping the heavy grains of beard that had gone unshaven since morning. His hand guided her mouth to hers. Pleasure filled him so completely that he could feel his body desperately yearning to have her.

"I love you," she whispered between kisses. "I've loved you since I first met y..."

His lips crushed hers, smothering not only her words but the emotion itself. He pulled away and fished a condom out of his pocket.

She looked at it and then at him.

He tried to read her. In his best John Wayne voice, he said, "I come prepared."

She smiled a demure smile.

"You okay with this?" he asked.

She nodded then unzipped her jacket.

So did he.

Oblivious to the chill, they removed their clothing.

He kissed her and then gently laid her down. He struggled to put on the condom then turned to her and stole tastes of her neck, her collarbone, the hollow of her throat, down her silky body, deep tastes, determined to leave nothing unclaimed. "Your skin is so soft," he murmured. "I can't stop myself from touching you."

"I don't want you to..." she moaned, her body trembling.

His nerves sang with incandescent heat. "You're all I ever wanted."

"You're all I ever need," she said.

"I am a newcomer to this," he said.

"Me, too," she said, clinging to him.

His body was slick with need, burning, burning everywhere. He was on fire. "Am I hurting you?"

"Sh-h-h..." Her hips surged upward. She made a sob-like sound, hoarse with lust then mutual climax.

He held her afterwards, until her trembling eased and her breath came evenly. Genuinely concerned, he asked, "Did I hurt you?"

"A little," she mumbled, "but it was worth it. It was perfect."

He pulled her away from him and looked into her eyes. Her face was wet with tears. He nudged away each tear with his thumbs then smiled at her and kissed her forehead. "I knew this would happen. My whole being was drawn to you since the first moment I saw you."

She laughed a little laugh. "Guess it was fate." Taking in a deep breath, she stretched out her arms. "I feel so crazy-happy. Wish it would last forever. Wish you didn't have to go."

"Well, my dear," he said, snagging their clothes. "We'll be here all night if we aren't sensible." He handed her a crumpled mass. "It's getting dark, so either we won't find our way out of this enchanted forest or we'll freeze to death."

"Maybe both," she said.

I trudged out to the barn, worried that Brad and Sky had not returned, pretending to be checking on the barn cats. It was dark and the cold got to me. I worried more about them. Then I heard: "I truly love you, Sky. Marry me."

"When you get back," she said. "I'll be graduated by then.

"We'll invite everyone - the whole town!" Brad said. "By now, you must be used to all the galas."

"Just come back safe and sound," she said.

In his John Wayne voice, he said, "Yes, ma'am."

Hiding behind the barn door, I held back a tearful chuckle.

Well, as much as we want it to, time won't stand still for anybody. Morning dawned and Brad was off to Active Duty, leaving me with two bawling women moping about my home. I tried to keep myself in a good way, so I could sway them toward the positive. Gradually I succeeded in getting faltering smiles.

Another snowstorm smacked the countryside. Everyone pitched in, shoveling mounds of snow that surely would last till spring. The plow was already rigged from the first snow, so I got out and cleared around the house and barn. Then I handed the plow over to Ron and Craig, who cleared access to the fields for the cows and riding paths for Sky and me. Being so busy kept us from dwelling on Brad's absence.

We had an unusually snowy January. Even so, Sky and I managed to ride Misty and Sarge every day.

The school was closed only one day, which made Sky happy. She was hell-bent-for-leather to graduate on time - with honors, no less. Nope, Sky was not about to miss one iota of school. So I put chains on the old Buick and off she went.

CHAPTER TWENTY-FIVE

I hired a new man and made Craig foreman. I, also, hired a high school senior named Casey to work afternoons and weekends and to cover the month of February. Craig was taking his vacation the first two weeks of February and then Bruce was taking vacation the last two weeks of February. Sky and I worked quite a lot during that time. Thankfully, Casey turned out to be an excellent worker. He even managed to come in mornings before going to school. He was a good student and would be graduating with Sky.

She worked mornings, too, and got to be close friends with Casey. He asked her for a date. She told him, "No. We can only be friends. My boyfriend Brad is in Afghanistan. We're promised to each other."

Prom was coming up in May. Mary and Billie were planning to go. Sky wanted to, but felt she shouldn't go without Brad. "Go with me," Casey said, "as friends."

"Geez, I don't know," Sky said.

"Well, think on it," he said. "But decide in the next couple of days, because that's when ticket sales end."

So Sky called up Lisa. "What I should do? I don't want Casey to think we can ever be more than friends."

"If he thinks such a thing after you told him Brad is your one and only, well, that's his problem," Lisa said. "Just remember, senior prom happens only once in a lifetime."

So Sky went dress shopping with Mary and Billie. It was an exciting time and Sky was pleased she decided to go with Casey.

After school one day, she told me about a lecture that had been held in the auditorium. A young man with a prosthetic leg had given a talk on drinking and driving. "He was drinking on the day of his prom," she said.

"Let me guess," I said. "He smashed up his car."

She nodded. "His date died. He showed slides of the scene. It was horrible. That guy is lucky he only lost his leg."

I tisked. "Worst of all, he has to live the rest of his life knowing that, because of his drinking, a beautiful young girl died."

"He asked us to sign a form, promising never to drink and drive," she said. "Everyone I know signed it."

On the second Saturday in May, prom was held, and I was ready with my camera when Casey came to pick up Sky. As he handed her a wrist corsage, he said, "You are the most beautiful creature on earth."

"I second that," I said.

Ignoring the compliments, she said, "You look stunning in that tux, Casey. Come on, Dad, take the pictures."

I waited up and was shocked when they got home and her dress was torn. I grabbed him by his shirt, winding up, poised to punch him out.

She grabbed my arm. "Casey didn't do it!"

"You better tell me real quick what happened or I'll…"

"Okay, okay!" Sky cried. "It's like this: I went into the ladies room. Mary followed me and told me Todd was acting weird and mean and she knew he had been drinking. She could smell it on his breath. She didn't know what to do, so I told her that Casey and I would take her home."

I let go of Casey's shirt. He sighed with relief and so did she. Then she continued, "I thought maybe one of Todd's friends would take him home. Anyways, Mary and I went to get Casey. We ran into Todd as we left and he got real nasty and grabbed Mary and hollered, 'I'm not drunk you…' Gosh, he called her so many bad names and then he says, 'I brought you here and I'm taking you home!'

"I grabbed Mary's hand and tried to run away, but then he grabbed my dress and tore it."

Casey spoke up, "Me and the other guys tackled Todd, but nothing we said or did simmered him down."

"So Casey and me and Mary took off," Sky said.

CHAPTER TWENTY-SIX

Friends were unable to convince Todd Stone not to drive home prom night, and after a brief struggle, were unable to take away his keys. So the inevitable happened: his car smacked into a tree. Airbags saved his life, but his injuries were serious enough to land him in the hospital for two weeks and then in a convalescing center for another four weeks of intense physical therapy.

Thank God, Mary had sense enough not to get into a car with an incapacitated driver. For the life of her though, she could not understand why Todd signed that form about not drinking and driving and then went ahead and did just the opposite. Several of their graduating class who visited him in the hospital asked him about it. "I was stupid," he said. "Just plain stupid. Worse of all, I can't even remember driving home after the prom. Did I get Mary home okay?"

When Sky heard about that, she said, "He should give the don't-drink-and-drive talk to next year's graduating class."

As for Mary, she never forgave Todd for spoiling prom night. She wanted nothing more to do with Todd Stone.

Spring weather was so perfect that every night after supper Sky and I rode the horses. She told me she and Brad were in love and planned to marry after Active Duty. I was pleased, especially now that her married name was going to be Brendan. "But I feel guilty," she said. "Here I am horse-back riding. It's Brad's dream, and now, he's so far away, fighting for us and our country."

"Think of it this way," I said. "He had to go, one way or the other, and so through your emails - and mine - he still gets the pleasure of being around horses. I bet that even in his dreams, he sees himself riding off into the sunset with you."

Sky giggled. "Gosh, Dad, you're such a romantic."

CHAPTER TWENTY-SEVEN

We didn't hear much from Brad for a few days. We shouldn't complain; at least we got emails. Soldiers of long ago and their families didn't have such luck. Still in all, Brad seemed okay. We told him about the prom and sent him pictures of Sky in her gown. We let him know about the graduation ceremony on the second Friday in June and to expect pictures of that.

Sky bought home her year book and we leafed through it together. I thought the publisher did a great job with it.

One week away from the final day, I heard a car drive up. I got up to see who it was just as a knock came at the door. My heart dropped out of me, for there stood two men in uniform. I wanted to scream out to Sky, but the words didn't come.

"Sir, are you Francis Brendan?" One of the men asked; his voice firm yet soft.

"I-I am."

"I am sorry to inform you, sir that your son Brad has been seriously injured in a firefight in Afghanistan. As we speak, he is being airlifted to a hospital in Germany. If you wish, you and family members may visit him there." He handed me an envelope. "Here is information you will need. I regret having to bring you this news." He

and the other soldier stiffened then saluted me.
They turned on their heels and marched back to
their car.

I sucked in a trembling breath then turned.
There was Sky. She had heard every last word. I
gathered her in my arms and she latched onto
me. Both of us were so very, very frightened.
"Brad is going to be okay," I managed to say. I felt
her shudder.

"I remember the day Mom got word that
Dad - my other Dad - was dead," she said. She
began to sob.

I held her, saying things I can't even recall,
things I thought might bring her some degree of
comfort. After a while, she hiccupped and
gradually calm down.

We went into the living room and sat on
the couch. I opened the envelope. Brad had
injuries to his legs and head; and it seemed to me
his entire body had been shattered. The
prognosis was scary. Reading about the hospital
in Germany, I said, "I have to go to him."

"Me, too," Sky said.

"What about finals?" I asked. "You have to
finish. What about graduation? The ceremony?"

She shook her head no. "I already have
enough credits to graduate, and no ceremony is
as important as Brad is. I'm going with you."

I booked a flight for both of us at two
o'clock the next day. So there we were, spending

Sunday night, packing suitcases. Terrible how quickly things change.

I called family members and that was hard. Hardest of all was calling Mom and Dad.

First thing, Monday morning, Sky drove to school and informed the principal of our plans. The principal assured Sky that she would graduate and her diploma would be mailed to her. The principal said she and the entire staff and student body would pray for Brad's speedy recovery.

I spoke to my farmhands, which included Casey who then volunteered to work full time while Sky and I were gone. My foreman, Craig, would be taking it all on his shoulders. I told all of them, "I have spoken to my brothers, and they have offered to help any way they can. Their phone numbers are posted on the bulletin board in the dairy. Please use Leo as last resort. This is his busy time on his farm. One other thing, Lisa is going to Germany with Sky and me."

CHAPTER TWENTY-EIGHT

The plane flight was too long. At first, Lisa wasn't sitting with us, so we kept getting up to chat with her, bothering the man seated on the aisle. He finally volunteered to switch places with Lisa. I don't know if that was a good move or not, because it wasn't long before I discovered Lisa wasn't the strong woman I thought she was. No, Lisa was not taking Brad's situation well at all. Most of the trip, she cried, and of course, Sky chimed in.

After arriving in Germany, we reset our watches and took a cab to the hospital. At the nurse's station, Lisa spoke right up, "I'm Lisa Brendan and..."

I cut her off, "And I'm Francis Brendan." I wanted the nurses to believe Lisa was Brad's mother, so there would be no doubt about her getting to see Brad. I pointed to Sky. "This is my daughter. The three of us are here to see Brad Brendan."

One of the nurses pressed a button on an intercom and said, "Family members to see Brad Brendan."

A voice came back, "Bring them in."

The nurse got to her feet. "Follow me, please." At a door marked, CRITICAL CARE, she pushed a button beside the door. We were buzzed in.

A woman, with thick braids that went halfway down the blouse of her blue scrubs, came up to us. "I'm Karen, Brad's day nurse. He is over here."

We trailed her through the middle of the Critical Care Unit that contained a dozen beds: six on one side, six on the other. Most of the green curtains surrounding each bed were open. Others were partially drawn. All the patients were linked to intravenous bags, which hung on stainless steel racks. Monitors beeped, registering heartbeats, blood pressure levels, and other bodily functions. The amount of bandaging was so great that we had no idea which patient was Brad.

"I paged his doctor," Nurse Karen said. "She will be here presently to speak with you."

Like other patients, Brad's head was wrapped in bandages. Additionally, his left leg was encased in a metal brace that was out in the open.

"Brad?" I said.

"I'm sorry, sir," Karen said. "Brad is in a medically induced coma."

The door buzzed. A woman dressed in white walked into the unit then introduced herself. "I am Doctor Jansen."

We all spoke at once, "Why was Brad in a coma? When will he wake up?"

Doctor Jansen held up a calming hand. "Brad has been put into a medically-induced coma, because the bullet that penetrated his forehead and the surgery to remove that bullet has caused swelling in his brain. Surgeons have removed part of his skull to relieve the pressure on his brain. The procedure is not unusual in cases like his. It minimizes brain damage."

"What about his leg?" I asked.

"Three bullets penetrated his left side. One damaged his hip; however, hip replacement will compensate for that. Two other bullets shredded his left leg. Unfortunately, he may lose that leg."

"When will you know for sure?" I asked.

"I will have a definite answer for you within a couple of days."

A mellow voice came over the loudspeaker, "Doctor Jansen, please. Doctor Jansen."

"I must go," she said. "Karen, will you kindly instruct this family on procedures?"

"Yes, Doctor Jansen," Karen said.

I didn't want Doctor Jansen to leave. I had too many unanswered questions, many of which I hadn't even thought of yet. But then, the doctor could do nothing for Brad at the moment - and some other patient needed her more.

"Visits must be kept to fifteen minutes at a time," Karen said. "The short amount of time is not just for Brad's benefit, but also to limit crowding in the Critical Care Unit. Not only does a crowd get in the way of patient care, but also, patients are just not up to visiting. I am always available during the day, so feel free to inquire about Brad's progress whenever you feel the need. I will introduce you to his evening and overnight nurses as soon as possible. They will be available to you when I am off shift, and any nurse working this unit will make every attempt to answer your needs at any time."

I took hold of Brad's free hand. "Okay my son, no more of this sleeping on the job. Sky, Aunt Lisa, and I have traveled a long ways and we expect you to behave like the strong Brendan you are. You will beat this. Then we'll all go back to the farm. You got chores, young man." I glanced at Sky and then at Lisa. Tears rolled down their cheeks. That's when I discovered tears were also rolling down mine.

"You must leave now," Karen said. "I will open the door for you, but please, when you come to the first nurses station, stop and give them your names, where you are staying, and telephone numbers to reach you at, should the need arise. One of the nurses at that station will set up a daily fifteen-minute schedule for each of you. Two visits a day per person, unless the doctor specifies differently."

Inside the hotel suite I had reserved, Sky, Lisa, and I caught up on sleep and tried to adjust to the time change. The miniature kitchen was not stocked with food, so we dined out our first meal. None of us could remember the last time we ate.

My next visit with Brad was at 2 o'clock. I cupped his hand in mine. "Hey, Brad, how ya doin'? Still lollygagging, I see." I told him about Dolly, the cows, the milk production, Sky and me riding the horses, the snowy winter.

"Time to leave," Karen said softly.

I kissed the back of his hand then rubbed it against my cheek. Without looking at her, I asked, "When will my son be woken up?"

"Expect him to be out for ten more days," she said.

With a heavy heart, I left and waited outside the hospital with Lisa while Sky went in to visit Brad. Sky came out. Lisa went in. We drew strength from talking with each other about our visits.

The next day, Karen told me the good news: "Brad is not going to lose his leg. He will need a lot of therapy though, and will be in a wheelchair for quite some time."

As days wore on and we felt more rested, we shopped for food, cooked, did a little sightseeing, and made numerous calls to the

States. So many people anxiously awaited news of Brad.

Then, on the tenth day, just like Karen told me, Brad woke up. His eyes were open when I walked into his cubicle. He frowned at the sight of me. I was taken aback. Brad didn't know who I was! I rushed out to find Karen. "I need to see the doctor."

A short time later, Doctor Jansen walked into the cubicle. "Do not to be disturbed by his confusion," She said. "It is entirely expected after an injury to the brain. The swelling is subsiding, which is the reason medication to keep him comatose has been withdrawn, thereby allowing him to awaken. Time is needed now for his brain to repair itself. You son will recognize you within days, but please remember, it will take months for him to return to his former self. One month from now, we expect to airlift him to a hospital in the States for physical therapy. As soon as he recognizes you, I suggest you stay only a couple more days. He has us to help him now and the physical therapy he will go through here will fill his days. Squeezing in visitors will be difficult."

CHAPTER TWENTY-NINE

Finally, Brad recognized me. Odd how one moment he didn't know me and then the next moment, he looked at me - really looked at me. "Dad! What are you doing here?"

"I've been here for weeks, son."

"No way. But hey, it's great seeing you, Dad. So why are you here? Did you want to see me in action? Well, war isn't all that interesting."

Sky and Lisa walked in. When I sent them a questioning look, Lisa said, "Karen came outside to get us. She thought that now Brad is awake, it might help him to he see us all together."

"Hi, Brad," Sky said, leaning over to kiss him.

He squinted at her, as if seeing her for the very first time, as if he might pull away from her. "Hey, where am I anyways?"

"You're in a hospital in Germany, Brad," Sky said. "You were injured in a firefight."

Lisa spoke up, "We needed to be here with you. Nobody's keeping me away from my nephew."

Brad appeared even more puzzled. Evidently, pieces of the firefight, pieces of us flashed in his head, because his agitation grew.

Karen stepped up to explain, as only Critical Care nurses can, what had happened to him. Then she turned to us. "Brad needs to rest, so please come back this afternoon at your regularly scheduled blocks of time." She led us out of the Critical Care Unit then said, "The Psych Nurse will talk to Brad as soon as she's free."

During my next fifteen-minute visit, Brad appeared more like his old self, and in the days that followed, he did so well that Lisa and I decided to go home, leaving Sky with him. A month later the doctor decided Brad was ready to be sent to a special hospital in northern Texas for ongoing physical therapy. So Sky came home.

I bought a Jeep, leaving the old Buick for Sky, and headed to Texas. Arriving just as Brad checked in, I was terribly distressed at how beat he looked. He appeared to be on the verge of crying. I pressed the call button and waited several moments. No response. I stepped out into the hall. Not a soul in sight. "For crying out loud!" I shouted. "Where is everybody?"

A male nurse came out of one of the rooms. "Please, sir! Lower your voice!"

I gathered myself together. "Sorry. It's just that my son just arrived and he's in pretty tough shape."

"I will see to him right away, sir," the nurse said, hurrying to his room. "We've had so many new arrivals that we just didn't get to him."

Brad was sobbing. When he saw us, he turned away. "I'm sorry. I'm sorry…"

"I am the one who should apologize," the nurse said. He unhooked the chart from the foot of the bed then scanned the pages. "Someone should have been here when you arrived. Are you in pain?"

Brad clenched his teeth.

"I'll get your medication." The nurse hurried out of the room.

I took his hand. "You'll be right as rain in two shakes of a lamb's tail."

The nurse rushed back, a syringe in his hand. "This will ease the pain," he said while injecting a heavy dose of morphine into Brad's arm.

Brad's eyes drooped. Then he slept.

I pulled up a chair next to his bed and sat there, watching him and at times, the television.

After he awoke, we talked for half an hour. I gave him a cell phone. "I programmed all the numbers I could think of. Give Sky a call. She's anxious to hear from you. As for me, I'm off to get me some supper. Then it's off to bed. As for you, my son, get some rest." I left him talking to Sky.

My hotel was not far from the hospital. Nearby was an Italian restaurant, so I stopped there first. What a terrific meal of lasagna I had. I complimented the chief while paying the waitress. Her eyes popped at my generous tip.

Next day, Brad was a new person. "The flight was horrible," he said. "Every bone in my body ached like the dickens. If it's possible to croak because of a plane trip, I would have right there and then. Oh, and thanks again for the phone, Dad. Talking to Sky helped a lot."

I was anxious to get back to the farm and when I did, it was on a Monday. Lisa was at the house with Sky and Dolly. "How come you're not at work?" I asked, giving her a hug.

"I wanted to see that you got home okay and to find out about Brad."

I got hugs from Sky and Dolly. Then the endless questions began. I assured them he was getting better every day.

"Okay, if I take the Buick and go see him?" Sky asked.

"It's yours to do with as you please," I said. "But I think it's best if you wait. Let him get settled in and get in some physical therapy. The nurse says Brad's going to be sore at first, and well, you know, Brad, how embarrassed he gets about showing weakness."

She twisted up one side of her face and nodded. "Okay. I'll go when Brad says so."

On August 30th, Brad got a roommate. "Nice to have company," he said, introducing himself.

"I'm Mac Burns," the new guy said.

"Is Mac a nickname?" Brad asked.

"Stands for MacKensie, which is my mother's maiden name. I've been Mac since a baby. So what's landed you here?"

"I took a bullet to the head, one to the hip, and two in my left leg. How about you?"

"Me and a bomb faced off. Lost my left leg. I got fitted with a prosthetic leg, so I'm here to learn to use it."

"Guess I'll be here longer than you," Brad said. "Where you from?"

"Houston. My wife is there, working, and can't come. My folks might come...sometime."

"My girlfriend is due here tomorrow," Brad said. "We live in Oklahoma, only a couple hours' drive from here."

When Sky walked in the next day, Brad was at physical therapy. She was astonished about how pushy Mac was.

"Hi cutie," he said. "You don't want that horse's ass when I'm here."

To her relief, the male nurse wheeled Brad into the room. "It's about time you showed up," Mac spouted. "This vision of beauty didn't know you are a horse's ass."

"Watch your mouth," Brad snapped.

"I second that," the nurse said. "Any more language like that and I'll wash your mouth out with soap."

As Sky gave Brad a big hug and a kiss, he whispered, "This is the first time that guy's talked like that. Ignore him, okay?"

After being settled into bed, he and Sky talked for quite some time. He squeezed her hand. "I love you so much, Sky. You don't know how anxious I am to get home and really, really show you."

Some familiar voices reached their ears and then Nanny and Poppy walked in. After much hugging and kissing, Brad introduced Mac.

"How is it that you are engaged and you share the same grandparents?" Mac asked. After getting an explanation, he said, "I think you should consider yourselves brother and sister. That way, I get a shot at this beautiful lady."

"Thought you said you was married," Brad said.

Mac snorted. "I neglected to tell you that while I was over there, fighting for our country, my wife found herself a lover and divorced me."

They all were shocked and felt deeply sorry for Mac. Now Brad and Sky understood his strange behavior.

"Well, Brad," Nanny said, "I am so pleased you are doing so well! Much better than I ever imagined! So have you and Sky set the date?"

"We were just getting to that when you walked in," Brad said.

Sky blushed.

Poppy rolled his eyes. "What about plans to raise cattle and horses?"

Mac piped up, "Hey, my Uncle Andrew raises cattle in Montana. I spent summers, working his ranch. I even learned how to rope newborn calves from a horse. Ah, those were the days. Hire me! I can be had for beans!"

"Uhm…" Brad stammered.

"Listen, man, I can rope and wrangle with the best of 'em!"

Brad and Sky exchanged looks. "Sure. Why not," Brad said. "When we're out of the service and back on our feet."

"Seems like you know more about ranch life than we do," Sky said.

Mac shrugged. "Maybe I can get my Uncle Andrew to lend a hand."

CHAPTER THIRTY

Brad and Mac became close friends, boosting each other up when either one was down and thinking they might never go home.

Mac's parents visited. Brad sensed coldness toward their only child. Perhaps that was due to them being focused on their careers. Mac's father, a contractor known for building large communities, rarely found time for his wife and son. Mac's mother didn't seem to mind though; she was wrapped up in her Event's Planning business. They stayed half an hour. After they left, Mac said, "I'm surprised either one of them found time to visit me. I think their main concern was to speak to my medical team and find out when I can travel back to Houston. But I'm a big boy now. I'll go where I want to go. You can bet the trip here took too much of their precious time."

"So that's why you're so interested in settling in Middle instead of going back to Houston," Brad said.

"You lucked out when you got a new Dad complete with aunts, uncles and cousins when you were eleven," Mac said.

"Not to mention later on when I got Sky."

Later on, Brad emailed me: Mac isn't looking forward to going home. I want to make him a partner in our cattle-raising plan. Give Mac a call, will you, and make him an offer?

I emailed back: Even before you yourself are heading home?"

Brad emailed: "Yes. Give Mac a place to bunk and put him to work in the dairy until I get there.

I was glad to do as Brad wished; and Mac was ecstatic, as if he had just been given a $100,000 a year job. A week later, he was released.

Brad felt bad, not only because he would miss Mac but also because he wanted to go home.

As it turned out, Mac earned every dime of his pay. He did everything I asked him and more with unbelievable enthusiasm. However, he rejected the room in the house I offered him. "That's too good for me. How about if I finish the space above the horse stalls for a bunkhouse?"

I chewed it over then said, "I can't see any reason not to."

Mac dived into the project. Then he bought himself a horse and a length of topnotch rope.

Sky and Mary remained friends. Mary, having no desire to go to college, had taken a job at an insurance and real estate office run by two women. She loved the work and her life in general. Evenings found Sky and Mary playing Monopoly, Clue, or some other game, usually at the kitchen table.

One night, Mac came in and ended up having a grand old time, playing Monopoly with the two girls. The three yelped and giggled. "We should be ashamed of ourselves," Sky said. "This game is for kids."

"Really?" Mac asked. "I never played it when I was a kid."

"My mother and grandmother played games with me all the time," Mary said.

"Nobody ever played with me," Mac said.

"That's awful," Mary said. She glanced at her watch. "Gosh, look at the time! I got to go!"

Mac jumped to his feet. "Say, what about you and me going out to eat sometime? And then a movie?"

"Gosh, I haven't gone to a movie in a long time," Mary said.

Sky didn't waste one minute before emailing Brad about the new lovers: From here on, we must consider Mary and Mac a couple.

Brad emailed back: Mary will be good for Mac. He's such a great guy. Those two deserve to be happy. Here's more good news: I'm being sprung!

Sky clasped her hands then emailed: When?

Next week!

I can't wait!
Let's get married, Sky!
Okay!
When?
Whenever!
How about October 15th?

CHAPTER THIRTY-ONE

"It's the end of August, Sky."

"So what, Dad?"

"That doesn't leave much time to prepare for an October wedding."

"D-a-d. Two months is more than enough time."

Dolly rolled her eyes at our bickering. "Actually, October is only month and a half away."

I crossed my arms and hooked my chin. "So there!"

Sky waved us off. "I'll get the whole family and Middle to help. Hope the weatherman cooperates, so we can have an outdoor reception. I have to get Aunt Lisa to help with my gown and also with the bridesmaids' gowns. I'm asking Mary to be my Maid of Honor and Mac will be Brad's Best Man."

"It'll be my job to help Brad with the tuxedo rentals," I said.

"And the flowers," Dolly added.

"Just think," Sky said, dreamily. "I'm going to be a Brendan."

I called Mom and Dad and gave them the good news. Then I went out to tell the farmhands, but Mary was there, so I didn't say a word except to tell her that she and Mac had to go talk to Sky right away. I followed them back to the house, just to see their reaction.

Sky was on the phone, talking to Lisa when we walked into the kitchen. It wasn't long before Mary and Mac got the gist of the conversation. They looked at each other then jumped around like jumping jacks.

Brad came home the following week. Happiness overflowed in the Brendan household - and for that matter, all over town! Ever since Brad arrived at the age of eleven, Middle had coddled him as if he were their own. Now that he had been wounded in action, townsfolk couldn't do enough to help him. They stepped right up and arranged his wedding to Sky.

Mac was amazed to see the turn out, lining the main road, cheering Brad as I drove him into town from the airport. I had rented a snazzy convertible. Sky, Mary, and Mac had come with me. Flags waved. Tidal waves of whistling, clapping, and yelling erupted at the sight of Brad. "Holy Smokes, Dad!" he exclaimed. "Feels like I've been gone forever!"

When we drove into our driveway, Dolly raced out to meet us. She kissed him again and again, before allowing Mac to wheel him into the house. She whispered to me, "Brad looks exhausted."

"Probably because of you smooching all over him like that."

In the downstairs bedroom we had prepared for him, I helped him to the bathroom and then into pajamas. "It's been a big day, Brad. A snooze with do you good." I helped him into bed. "We have plenty of time to get you back in the swing of things."

Two hours later, we were surprised to see Brad standing with crutches, in the living room door. I stood up. "I wasn't aware that you were able to maneuver so well on those things."

"I'm not all that good at it," Brad said.

"You'll get better," Sky said.

He winked at her. "I intend to do away with them before you and I make it to the church."

Mac piped up, "Didn't I promise you, I'd coach you into tiptop shape?"

In the days that followed, Brad, Sky, and Mac talked me a blue streak about plans to enlarge the farm into a cattle and horse ranch. Sky was going to use the money she inherited from her mother. When I learned of their plan to build a house, I said, "There's a nice piece of land close to the pond. It's my wedding present to you."

"Wish Sky and I could ride out there and see it," Brad said. "I'm anxious to ride Sarge. With my problems walking, it's a great way for me to get around."

So Sky and Mac took Brad out to the paddock. While she got out a stepping stool, Mac walked Sarge out of the stall. Brad hobbled over to the stool on his crutches then maneuvered himself onto the stool. He handed Sky the crutches. Three times, he attempted to throw his leg over Serge's back. On the fourth try, he succeeded. He wiggled around and got comfortable. Mac helped to get Brads feet into the stirrups.

"Wow, you did it!" Sky exclaimed, scooping up the stool, just in case it was needed later. She attached it to the blanket on Misty's back then jumped on. "Let's go to the pond!"

"Come on, Sarge, let's go," Brad said as Mac trotted ahead on Major.

I couldn't help but think how amazing it was to see the three ride off together. Mac had gotten so adept with his prosthesis leg, at getting on his horse, and I believed Brad would do as well. This ride was going to do all of them a lot of good.

Brad told me later that when they got to the pond he wanted to dismount, but didn't know if he could handle it. He decided to try it, so Sky put the stool down then he threw his right leg over the saddle. He clutched the saddle as he slipped down to the ground. They were all amazed, him most of all. Not having his crutches with him, he leaned on Sarge while Sky spread the blanket on the ground. She and Mac helped him lower himself onto the blanket then Mac tied the horses to a nearby tree. "We can't stay too long," Mac said. "Mary and I have a date, but I want to ask you two something: Can I go in with the two of you on the cattle ranch? My grandmother left me a big trust fund."

"I'm all for making you an equal partner," Brad said. "How about you, Sky?"

"I certainly am."

Mac grinned. "With the three of us pitching in financially and working hard, we can do real good."

"I'll get Aunt Lisa to draw up a contract," Brad said.

"She'll want a name for the ranch," Sky said.

"How about the Sky Mac Brad Ranch?" Brad suggested.

"Perfect," she said.

Mac piped up, "Our cattle-brand should be SMBR."

CHAPTER THIRTY-TWO

The days before the wedding grew busier and busier while Brad worked harder and harder to train his legs to do his bidding. He was bound and determined to walk on the day of his wedding.

Meanwhile, a hired crew began to clear the trees for access to the pond. Brad and Sky were saddened to lose so many trees; however, they planned to replant some everywhere possible.

Lisa drew up corporation papers for the Sky Mac Brad Ranch. Then the new ranchers set up a bank account.

Nanny and Poppy arrived, joining family, friends, and the town in preparing for the wedding. The girls hunted for gowns then made sure the fit was perfect.

Uncle John's son, Jason, was going to be the ring bearer. Uncle Leo's twins were going to be junior bridesmaids. Billie was to be the adult bridesmaid, and of course, Mary was Maid of Honor. John's son Paul and Leo's son Chris were going to be ushers, and of course, Mac was Best Man.

On October 14th, the girls got their hair done and the guys went for haircuts. Gowns and tuxedoes got picked up. That evening, the rehearsal was held and afterwards, the rehearsal dinner. Everyone hung on the latest weather report. Surely, the day was going to be a dandy one.

Early on the morning of the ceremony, the air was crisp as crews set up tarpaulin, tables, chairs, and a host of other requirements. The air warmed up as the house filled with excitement.

At one forty-five, Nanny and Poppy smiled as their grandsons escorted them down the aisle of Saint Timothy's Church. Others were shown their places.

At one fifty-five, Brad walked unaided to the rail in front of the altar. Every step of the way, Mac was at Brad's side. Father Francis appeared; his palms and fingers touching in reverence. At the rear of the Church, I admired my daughter in her wedding gown. "I can't believe I have such a gorgeous daughter."

Sky blushed. "Thanks, Dad."

The twins strolled down the aisle, grinning ear to ear. Clearly, they had never felt so beautiful. Mary headed down. Danny followed. The wedding march started. "This is it," I said, linking Sky's arm in mine. She trembled all the way to Brad. I placed her hand in his then took my place beside Mom and Dad. Before I knew it, Sky was saying those time honored words: "I, Sky Marie Farmer, take you, Brad Louis Brendan, to be my lawfully wedded husband…"

My Sky was now a Brendan.

CHAPTER THIRTY-THREE

The reception overflowed with laughter, dancing, and food. I wished for it to last the entire night. I wished for Sky and Brad to laugh and dance and dance and laugh. Hours passed. Suddenly, Sky shrieked, "Brad!"

As gasps rippled throughout the hall, I spotted Brad lying in a heap on the floor. Sky was kneeling next to him. His face was gray as a January afternoon. I raced over to them and dropped to the floor. Leo plopped next to me. John and Mac skidded onto the floor on other side of Brad. As we braced Brad up, into a seated position, Dolly tugged Sky out of our way. I loosened his collar I heard Doc Stone bellowing, "Out of my way!" I saw him elbowing his way through guests. "Out of my way!"

My heart thumped. "He's unconscious, Doc! He's unconscious!"

Doc lifted one of Brad's eyelids. Then he took his pulse. "Let's get him into the house."

As Leo, John, Jerry, and I lifted Brad, Dolly and Sky ran ahead and opened the door. The crowd swelled along with us. As we entered the house, Dolly hustled people back. Sky trailed behind us. In the downstairs bedroom, we lowered him onto the bed. "Help me get these clothes off him, Frank," Doc said.

"What's wrong with him?" Sky cried.

Doc and I ignored her, not to be mean though. While stripping him down, I spotted his leg. So did Doc. I frowned at Doc. He frowned back.

Brad moaned.

"He's coming around," Doc said.

"Take it easy, son," I said.

"Wha...what happened?"

"You leg wounds are festering," Doc said. "You got a dreadful case of blood poisoning."

"Blood poisoning?" Brad echoed.

"You're going to have to stay off of that leg," Doc said as Dolly rushed in with his black bag. "And stay out of that barn! Away from all those animals and germs!"

"N-no," Brad protested, trying to sit up.

It didn't take much for me to push him back onto the bed. "You need time to heal, son."

"I'm aware you have big plans," Doc said. "But you're going to lose that leg - and your life - if you don't follow my orders."

"Let me up, Dad..."

I held him down.

"Now you listen to me, Brad Brendan," Sky snapped. "I'm your wife now, you hear? And I say you will stay in that bed and let that leg heal! Or so help me, I will put you in the grave myself!"

We gawked at her hovering over us. I for one was not about to tangle with her!

"You heard me, Brad Brendan," she snarled. She turned to Doc. "Now tell me, Doc, how long is it apt to be before that leg is healed?"

Doc sputtered, "Likely...six months, er, Mrs. Brendan."

"Six months?" Brad yelped.

Sky shook her finger at him. "Brad!"

"But..."

Again that finger. "You can make all the plans you want on the computer and figure them this way and that, and you will also keep a diary of all you do *and* your progress. Remember when Mary volunteered to help? As long as she didn't need to be on a horse? Well, you are going to train Mary to be your office manager."

Brad pondered his new wife and that finger she was pointing at him. "What about the road to the pond?"

I spoke up, "I know what has to be done. I'll get equipment and a crew on it, first thing in the morning." I squinted at Doc Stone. "Nothing saying Brad can't take a ride in my Jeep, once in a while, and check on things, right, Doc?"

"If the healing goes well," Doc said. "Then again, surviving his new wife is another thing entirely."

Brad accepted the inevitable much better than I thought he would. He appointed Mac, Site Manager. Mac asked his Uncle Andrew to come from Montana and provide much-needed sage advice about ranching. Mac planned on having Andrew bunk in the loft with him.

One day, Sky, Mac, and I were discussing the business with Brad. She was sitting on the bed, holding Brad's hand. I reclined in the rocking chair while Mac perched upon the window sill. "Damn shame, you two aren't on your honeymoon," Mac grumbled.

Brad squeezed Sky's hand. "I have my new wife and we're together; that's all that matters."

"As long as you follow doctor's orders," Sky added.

He winked at her.

"Now, don't you go starting your charming ways on me, Brad Brendan," she said.

"Yes, ma'am," he said in his best John Wayne voice. "Anyhow, guys, I installed a Quicken disk to keep track of our financial activities. Now we have constant and accurate records, everything we need. Mary's training is going great. No problem with her taking over when I get out of this stinking bed."

"Did you tell them the news, Mac?" Mary asked while walking into the bedroom. Before he got the chance to say one word, she gushed,

"We're getting married on April 18th! Mom and Grammy are already full steam ahead with wedding planning!"

Sky leaped off the bed, squealing. She latched onto Mary then the two leaped about like giddy schoolgirls. Suddenly, Sky broke loose. "Call your Mom and Grammy! They have to come for supper! Oh! We have to help Dolly! We need to set extra places!"

At supper, Brad said, "After Mac and Mary get married, Mary should be an equal partner in the business."

"I'll withdraw another $100,000 from my trust fund," Mac said, "and put it in the account."

"Mac, no," Mary said. "It's not right for you to clean out your trust fund."

"Yes, it is," Mac said. "We need lots of money to plant this seed and I *can* afford it. My grandfather left me a trust of $750,000, and my attorney told me this ranch is a great place to put my money. We can get his help to check out anything we need investigated. No gangster is going to come along and play *us* like fools."

Sky turned to Mary. "Would you like to wear my wedding gown? I understand if you rather not wear a second hand dress."

"Are you kidding?" Mary cried. "I'd never call your gorgeous gown a second hand dress! Wow! You'd really let me wear it? I'd be ever so careful not to..."

Sky butted in, "Hey, accidents happen; and if something does, I promise not to get angry. So what do you say we go upstairs after supper and you can try it on?"

Dolly piped up, "If adjustments are needed, I'm happy to do them."

Only the length needed shortening; other than that, the dress fit Mary perfectly. "Look at you," Sky said. "You are even more beautiful in it than I was. Your shiny dark hair looks fabulous against all that white."

A dreamy look enveloped Mary. "Imagine me...living here on the farm...with Mac...and the rest of you..."

"The loft he created over the stables is nicer than any house I know," Sky said. "And that generator he put in sure saved the farm last month when that idiot drove into the electric pole west of here."

"Mac wants to save up and build us a house," Mary said.

"You're not moving away, are you?"

"No way! Never!"

CHAPTER THIRTY-FOUR

"**U**ncle Andrew is married," Mac said, chomping on a sandwich.

"And her name?" Dolly asked.

"Elizabeth," he said.

"How come she's not coming with him?" Sky asked.

Mac shrugged. "Maybe he decided to make a vacation out of it."

"A vacation," Dolly echoed. "And Elizabeth is okay with her husband taking a vacation without her?"

"She likes to be called Bess," he said.

"To you, she's Aunt Bess," Dolly said.

"Uh-huh."

"Is it okay if Dolly and I invite your Aunt Bess to come with him?" Sky asked.

"Sure," Mac said.

And so Dolly and Sky called Bess; and while they were at it, volunteered to show Bess around Middle. Upon hanging up, Dolly rubbed her hands together. "Well, they'll be arriving in two weeks. We don't have much time, Sky. That large bedroom upstairs needs clean sheets and..."

"Hold on, Dolly," Sky said. "Mac's planning on Uncle Andrew staying in the loft."

"That's no place for a woman like Bess!"

"Leave it alone, Dolly," I said, walking into the room. She gawked at me. "Yes, I heard the whole conversation, start to finish - from the bathroom. Go ahead and make all the plans you want to make their stay comfortable, but it's Mac's choice where his family bunks. Not to mention, that loft is fit for royalty."

Dolly harrumphed.

"On another note," I said. "I was reading the newspaper and noticed an ad for rental vans that accommodate wheelchairs."

"A van," Sky said. "Brad's been feeling bad about not going out to the pond."

"Well, I don't know if a van can do that much," I said.

"It can handle the new road to the pond," Sky said.

"I'll look into renting a van," I said.

The rental van arrived two days before Andrew and Bess. My first thought was: Am I really going to let Brad drive this thing all by himself?

Mac pointed out the lift lever that would help Brad get into the driver's seat. "You can drive any time you want to."

Brad looked skeptical. However, he was happy to use the rear lift that picked him up, and the wheelchair, and safely deposited him in the back of the van. "I can go places in a heartbeat!"

"Let's go!" Mac exclaimed.

Brad gave Mac a sidelong look. A smile blossomed on his face. "Yeah! Let's go, Dad!"

We headed off to see Leo and family. When we got there, Brad got himself out of the van and then his wheelchair. While touring the farm, Leo introduced Mac to the hands.

"Well, look at you, little cutie," Mac said.

At first, we thought Mac was talking to a woman, but then following his line of sight, we spotted kittens.

"Mary would like that pitch black one," Mac said.

"It's yours for the taking," Leo said.

"Awesome," Mac said. "Come to Daddy, Ebony."

Watching Mac chase down the black kitten, Brad said to Leo, "Looks like Mary just got her first wedding present."

Leo hooked his chin. "Come on. Take a gander at my strawberry patch. There are oodles of them this year. There's so many, me and the hands can't pick them all. Just this morning, I put a pick-your-own ad in the Middle Bulletin."

"Will you look at all the strawberries?" Mac exclaimed, coming through the gate with the black kitten tucked in his arms.

"Pick all you want," the twins said in unison.

"I'll pay you if you pick a gallon of them for me," Mac said.

They glanced at Leo. "Okay, Daddy?"

Leo chuckled. "Of course."

"Mac is a beginning cook," Brad said while happily maneuvering his wheelchair toward Leo's house.

"Dolly has the patience of Job," I said.

Mac rolled his eyes. Then he said, "I'm fascinated with the idea of farm fresh fruits and vegetables."

"Count on all you want, Mac," Leo said. "When they come in season, that is."

"Free?" Mac said. "Now that's just plain stealing."

"Nah," Leo said. "The amount of produce we sell or use around here is piddling compared to what we plant. We have to, in case of drought, floods, locusts…"

In the house, everyone helped themselves to the bowl of fresh strawberries adorning the kitchen table. "This reminds me about a story I heard about a minister visiting an old lady," Mac said. "Beside the chair he was sitting on was a bowl of peanuts. As they talked, he munched on those peanuts and ended up eating them all. When he apologized, the old lady waved him off, saying, 'Not to worry. Those peanuts were too hard for me to chew on anyway. Besides, I already sucked off all the chocolate."

"Yuck!" the kids shrieked as adults laughed.

Since we were out and about, Brad suggested we stop at This And That and pick up supplies for the black kitten. He wheeled into the store, which gave Abby a thrill. So much so that she put the closed sign in the door and went to lunch with us at Louie's Pizza and Sub Shop next door.

After that, we stopped off to see John at the Sheriff's Office. By that time, Brad was plumb tuckered out. "You didn't overdo yourself, did you?" I asked.

Brad grinned. "I don't care if I did."

As we were leaving, Mac glanced across the street at the insurance office where Mary worked. "Look, she's in the window! She's waving at us! Let's go say hello!"

When we climbed back into the van, Mac said, "Know what, you guys? I got a real good feeling coming at me. Man! Did I luck out when I met Brad or what? This town and the people in it make me feel a kind of happiness I never felt before. It's like their all my relatives or something. Why don't I feel this way around my parents? You know, I feel sorry for them. They're missing all this. And why aren't they more like Uncle Andrew and Aunt Bess? How could my mother have been brought up a MacKensie, just like Uncle Andrew, and end up so different? Wonder if Dad changed her nature? Or is it their careers that did it? I'll be so happy when Uncle Andrew and Aunt Bess get here. I knew they'll love it here, too."

When we got home, Mac told us about a message on his answering machine. "Uncle Andrew and Aunt Bess will be arriving Saturday at the airport at 10:00 AM. They plan to hire a car and think they'll have no trouble finding their way here."

At supper Dolly was all aflutter. "Saturday is only two days away! This place just isn't ready for company!"

Everybody knew that she had everything ready - and more. You'd think it was her relatives coming to visit. I kind of figured she was looking forward to being with a woman her own age.

"Can't wait to talk to Uncle Andrew," Brad said. "There's so much to learn about cattle ranching."

"Uncle Andrew and I are going to explore the area beyond the pond," Mac said. "He's arranged with some big sporting goods store to outfit us with three or four days camping gear, which includes a two person tent, a two burner cooker, and c-rations."

"You're staying overnight?" Brad asked.

Mac nodded. "It's the only way to see what's beyond the pond."

"Cows need lots of acreage," I said.

"Wish I could go along," Brad said.

"Me, too," Mac said.

"I don't suppose the cell phones will work way out there," I said.

"We'll try them," Mac said. "Maybe Uncle Andrew can get us walkie-talkies, just in case."

"Good idea," I said.

Brad changed the subject. "So Dolly. I don't want you to feel bad, but I really want to have a private talk with Uncle Andrew and Aunt Bess when they get here. So I'm having them come to the loft first."

"Perfectly understandable," Dolly said. "It's been a long time since you've seen them. Tell you what, I'll make up sandwiches and cookies and..."

Brad cut in, "And I'll make the coffee."

"You sure?" Dolly said. "You know I'll..."

"I make coffee every morning, Dolly; and if I do say so myself, it's pretty darned good."

CHAPTER THIRTY-FIVE

Just as Andrew and Bess pulled in, the twins were arriving with the strawberries they had picked for Mac that morning. And being an aspiring cook, Mac had made biscuits for strawberry shortcake. The dairy provided all the heavy cream needed for whipped topping.

Neither Andrew nor Bess looked like I had imagined them. Andrew was sturdily built. I guessed him to be in his early to mid forties. Bess might be his age, although she was built like a teenage boy. She wore a ponytail, jeans, and a colorful knit top.

Mac told me later how much he enjoyed his time in the loft with his aunt and uncle. After a brief tour, she told him, "This loft is just lovely. And you keep it so tidy - unusually tidy, I'd say, for a man."

"I can't stand a mess," Mac had said, picking up the black kitten. "This is Ebony. Kind of a wedding present I got for Mary."

"What a darling," Bess said, taking the kitten then cuddling him. "Oh, my, listen to him purr!"

They settled at the kitchen table, munching on Dolly's sandwiches and sipping the coffee Mac had brewed. After bringing each other up to date about their lives, Andrew said, "Your aunt and I are pleased you found a girl you plan to share your life with. When do we meet her?"

"Tonight," Mac said, taking the strawberry shortcake out of the refrigerator. "She'll join us for supper at the main house after work."

Andrew licked his lips. "That cake looks scrumptious!"

"Shame on you, Mac," Bess joked. "You know very well, I have a weakness for whip cream."

"Yours truly whipped it," Mac said. "The cows furnish all the dairy products needed around here. As you know, Leo's twins picked the strawberries, but I made the biscuits."

When Mac got up to clean off the table, Bess insisted on helping. While they washed the dishes, Andrew wandered outside then into the dairy, where I was preparing for the day's milk to be picked up. Andrew was full of questions, because his dealings with cattle were quite different from mine. I showed him how the milking was done and stored then explained Brad's thoughts about raising cattle in order to furnish milkers when the dairy needed them. "I'm not sure having cattle that take extra land and make extra work makes sense, but I'm sure those four kids will make a good business out of it. I certainly appreciate the help you're giving them and the Sky Mac Brad Ranch."

"You're right in thinking a lot of land is needed," Andrew said. "That's why Mac and I plan to ride out beyond the pond and camp out. It'll be interesting to see what's out there."

"Mac and I stored the camping gear you ordered in the shed near the stable," I said.

"I think one horse can carry it all," Andrew said. He seemed ill-at-ease. He cleared his throat then asked, "So, what do you think of Mac's intended?"

"He couldn't have found a finer girl," I replied. "Real down to earth - just like him. Sky and Mary have been tight since high school. I'm tremendously pleased those four kids are settling here."

CHAPTER THIRTY-SIX

As the milk tanker pulled out, I was talking with my foreman. That's when I heard Andrew say to Bess, "Mac's choice of wife concerns me."

"Now, Andrew," she said. "You haven't even met Mary yet. Give the girl a break."

He scratched his head. "Frank says she's down-to-earth. You know what that means, Bess: She's plain-looking; shy; humble with no get-up-and-go. That type won't keep Mac happy."

"You're doing it again, Andrew: Jumping to conclusions before you have the facts."

With a twinge of spitefulness, I watched a car pull into the farm. It parked in front of Mac's loft. I knew full well who it was. I motioned to the driver, a lovely girl, a girl I cared about almost as much as I cared about Sky. As she got out of the car, I hollered, "Hey, Andrew and Bess! Come on over. Mary's here!"

I noticed Bess elbowing Andrew. "Another one of your theories shot to hell," she muttered. "I'd say Mary is far from plain, wouldn't you? In fact, I'd say she is quite a looker."

"Aunt Bess! Uncle Andrew!" Mary gushed. "May I give you a hug?"

"I'd be disappointed if you didn't," Bess said; and as they did, she winked at Andrew.

When the MacKensies walked into my kitchen at suppertime, Sky and Dolly greeted them with hugs. "We're all so very happy to finally meet you two," Sky said. "You won't believe how itchy Brad and Mac have been to see you."

Dolly up and downed Bess. "My goodness, girl, were you a child bride?"

Bess giggled. "Don't tell anyone, but I am forty years old. So no, I was not a child bride."

Andrew changed the subject. "Bess and I were never able to have children of our own, so we doted on Mac from the day he was born. His parents were parents to their jobs."

"Now, please don't think we're faulting them," Bess said. "But we do love Mac like a son." She spotted Brad sitting in his wheelchair, Buddy by his side, both taking it all in. "You must be Brad." She went over and cupped his cheeks in her hands.

"Nice to finally meet you, Mrs. MacKensie."

She kissed him on his forehead. "We are so happy to be here. And everyone, please call me Aunt Bess." She pointed at Andrew. "And he's Uncle Andrew."

After the grand supper that Dolly and Sky served, Brad said, "Uncle Andrew, while the kitchen gets cleaned up, why don't I show you what I've been working on at my computer for Sky Mac Brad Ranch? When my leg heals and my doctor says it's safe from further infection, I'm handing over the computer end of things to Mary. She's far better at it than I am. I can't wait to get out in the fields."

When Mac and Mary walked into the office, Andrew spotted their linked hands. He didn't seem to like that much, and instantly became an interrogator. "Well, now, Mary, Brad tells me you are quite knowledgeable about computer work. How are you at dealing with financial aspects?"

"Actually, she's even better at that," Brad said.

Mary smiled.

"She's great at games," Mac said.

"Games," Andrew echoed, his face sour as a pickle.

Mary shrugged. "I like doing cryptograms. It's like I'm a spy trying to break codes. What I really like is Sudoku."

"She's awesome at everything," Mac said.

"In grade school, I enjoyed doing math in my head," she said. "Teachers were always encouraging me to take accounting courses and so I went to night school."

"Seems to me," Andrew said, "if indeed you were that good, it would have been a better idea for you to go to a college with a CPA major. Why didn't you?"

"Andrew!" Bess snapped, entering the room. Her eyes shot daggers at him.

We all were taken aback; although I was so proud of Mary and the way she stood up to Andrew. "I didn't want to saddle my mother or grandmother *or myself* with a big college bill," she said. "I know a lot of people who have done that and are having trouble paying it off. I'm quite happy I took the accounting course. I did real well at it; and now, I love my job. Plus I make extra money doing people's income taxes. I made a deal with my boss. I have use of the office and fork over two percent of what I earn. My boss told me I'm very valuable to the company. I get great raises. My boss even told me that if I ever considered a job offer from a different company, I should tell him, so my company has a chance to match the offer."

"My goodness," Bess said, putting an arm around Mary. "It seems your employers are afraid of losing you. I'd say, you have a good head on your shoulders, wouldn't you, Andrew?" He remained mum.

"There's nothing ordinary about my Mary," Mac said. "I am so blessed to have her."

"Come on, Andrew," Bess said. "It's getting late and we had a very long day." I suspected she was anxious to get her husband alone and give him what-for about putting Mary on the spot like that.

Shortly after dawn the next morning, I helped Brad to get dressed. He wanted to be there when Mac and Andy checked out the boxed camping gear. Nobody wanted any surprises. Good thing we did. A tent stake was missing. Luckily, I found one in the barn.

Andrew lit the camp stove. "Working fine."

"We got two pans with covers, a fry-pan, and a one-pint kettle," Mac said. "Here's some kind of packaged eggs I never seen before. Here's instant coffee and tea bags. Yuck. I'll bring coffee grounds. I make the best camp coffee, you know. Hey, look at all the metal dishes and utensils. Here's a sponge and a dishtowel; and liquid soap to wash dishes and other stuff. Towels. Facecloths. And a washbasin."

"You're going to need a mirror to hang on a tree," I said, "to shave with. Don't forget personal toilet articles."

"I need to pack a change of clothes, rainwear and boots," Mac said. Then he chuckled. "And surprise, surprise! Toilet paper! Can't forget that!"

Supplies also included a first aid kit, a hunting knife, a hatchet, boxes of matches, and paper for starting a fire.

"Dolly says she's making a huge sack of sandwiches and wrapping them in foil," I said.

"Big surprise," Mac said.

"Speaking about surprises," Andrew said. "I managed to get my hands on a field phone, the same kind soldiers use to keep in touch with command during battle. It's in my car."

Brad was ecstatic. "Now I'll be able to know what you're up to way out there!"

After checking out the horses, we came out of the barn and were surprised to see a horse-drawn wagon creaking toward us. It looked like something right out of an old west movie. "What in the world...?" Andrew sputtered.

"That's Uncle Leo and his horse Belle," Brad said as Buddy ran out to greet them.

"Leo uses Belle and the wagon to get supplies and crops in and out of his fields," Mac said.

Leo pulled Belle up in front of us. "I brought you something I bet you didn't even know you needed."

"What are you talking about?" Andrew asked, rather harshly.

Good-natured Leo sloughed off the tone. "Happy to meet you, Andrew. This wagon will get your supplies anywhere you need."

"It won't cross a pond," Andrew said.

"Sure it will, if the water level is low enough," Leo said. "Plus that pond in the woods is small enough. Belle can get this wagon around it in a heartbeat. So as it happened, the thought came to me in the middle of the night: Belle and this wagon is something Mac and Andrew might end up happy in having."

"Thanks, Leo," Mac said. "I was worried about packing so much gear on one horse."

I could almost read Mac's mind: How wonderful to have such caring family and friends who are always willing to help. I was thinking the same thing.

"A tarp is in the wagon," Leo said. "Throw it over everything to keep it dry and in the wagon whenever you go over bumps."

"I never knew a camping trip to go off without rain," I commented.

Leo rolled his eyes. "That's a fact."

"One more thing," Brad said, reaching into the pocket of his wheelchair. "Here's my video cam. Better take it or Sky will have my hide."

"None of us want you tangling with Sky," Mac said, grabbing the video cam.

Leo patted Andrew on the back. "Heather and I want you and Bess to drop in to see us when you get back. Have a great time."

Well, of course, the weatherman predicted rain during the night. Rain or shine, Mac and Andrew intended to leave at first light the next morning. So Mac pulled the wagon into the barn.

After bedding down, Belle, Misty, Sarge, and Major in their stalls, I helped to load gear into the wagon. "More than likely, there's plenty of grass for the horses," I said. "But here are three bags of oats, just in case."

CHAPTER THIRTY-SEVEN

Dolly was up at 5:30 a.m., cooking breakfast. So was everyone else, all wanting to see Mac and Andrew off. Buddy circulated, looking for treats.

The field phone was set up in the kitchen because usually, somebody was there. More than likely, Brad would be hovering over it.

Mac came in decked out in rain gear. "It's spitting out," he said, grabbing a muffin. He waved off the coffee Dolly offered. "I'm already on a caffeine overload."

"Did you pack up the duffle bag with all the extra stuff we talked about?" Andrew asked.

Brad nodded while chewing the muffin. He swallowed then said, "It's in the wagon, along with the other supplies, covered with the tarp."

Before long, the campers set out toward the misty forest. If not for the new road that ended at the pond, they would have looked like settlers of old. I prayed for the rain to stay light so as not to slow them down or worse, the wagon getting stuck in mud. At the slow rate they were going, they would reach the pond in forty-five minutes to one hour, which was right around the time Brad's cell phone rang. "Mac! Yeah, I hear you, but not very clear. Okay, we'll think on it. Yeah, I'll update everyone." He hung up then turned to the rest of us lollygagging around the kitchen, anticipating the call. "Mac says it didn't take long to set up the tent at the pond. The canopy flap at the entrance stops the rain from coming in. Andrew is rolling out the bed rolls. The field phone is next. He and Uncle Andrew think we should name the pond."

Our eyes wandered as we pondered a name. Finally, I said, "Just call it Small Pond."

"But what if tomorrow or the day after, they find more ponds?" Sky asked.

Mary spoke up. "And what if they're small?"

"Well, we can't name them all," Dolly said.

"Besides, they might not be on our land," I said.

The field phone buzzed. Brad snatched it up. "Yeah! You're coming in loud and clear, Uncle Andrew. Okay. I'll tell her." He turned to Dolly. "Your sandwiches were great."

Dolly clasped her hands over her heart and grinned ear to ear.

Further communications gave us visions of their progress:

After lunch and cleanup, clouds lifted. Leaving Belle to munch grass, Mac and Andrew rode Major and Sarge around Small Pond, surveying the topography. Mac took videos while Andrew sketched charcoal images. I was surprised to learn that Andrew was an artist, genuinely interested in the environment, and knowledgeable about plant life. He wasn't only sketching plants; he was labeling them, too. So I asked him, "Did you study plants?"

"I took several courses in Botany," Andrew replied. "I find it very interesting. I have numerous plant books back home. I brought one with me. It's my favorite handbook on plants. It helps to know which plants are edible. I just saw a False Solomon Seal."

"A favorite of bears," I said, recalling its sweet, sugary berry that had a seed in the middle. "The roots are starchy."

"Tell me they're not going to eat wild plants," Dolly said.

"No reason not to," I said. "Doing so preserves their supplies."

"They better be on the lookout for bears," Sky said.

"And poison ivy," Brad added. "Leaves of three - poison ivy!"

"I hope they steer the horses clear of it," I said.

Small pond was true to its name. On the other side of it, Mac and Andrew could see their campsite without any effort. Behind them was a hill, which they thought, may be considered a mountain. They asked me the name of it. Offhand, I didn't know.

Upon returning to camp, Mac and Andrew got a good laugh out of Belle sleeping standing up.

Mac lit the stove pilot light then got out a fry-pan and put it on a burner. He poured some oil into the pan then turned on the burner. He opened up cans of Spam, sliced potatoes, and corn. While frying the Spam and potatoes in the hot oil, he sprinkled them with salt, pepper, and garlic. He poured the corn in the smaller pot and when it was hot enough, he took the pot off the burner. He placed a kettle filled with water on the burner and waited for it to come to a boil. He added coffee grounds. The potatoes and spam browned nicely, so Mac shut off the both burners then plated the food. He passed one plate to Andrew then poured coffee into two cups, gently, so as to minimize grounds in the coffee. He handed a cup to Andrew then picked up the other plate and cup and stepped over to the folding chair beside Andrew.

"This grub is fantastic," Andrew said.

Mac laughed as he sat down. "Certainly isn't the fanciest."

"When you're hungry - and I *am* hungry," Andrew said. "Anything tastes good. However, this grub is way beyond good!"

"The person who is served supper is the one who lights the campfire," Mac said.

"I'm on it," Andrew said. "Tomorrow, I make supper. But just to let you know, I ain't much of a cook."

"So why don't I do all the cooking?" Mac said. "You be the cleanup man and fire-starter and make sure the fire is out when it's supposed to be."

"You won't see me complaining about any of that," Andrew said. "But we should keep a fire going every night to keep the varmints away. If either of us wakes up during the night and see the fire is low, we have to throw on a log. I'll gather up extra wood before I hit the sack."

Zipped into a sleeping bag, Mac babbled on and on, "I'm looking forward to seeing what we find at the base of that mountain. Mount MacKensie, that's what we'll call it. I sure do feel like an explorer. How about you, Uncle Andrew? Uncle Andrew?"

Snoring, coming from the other side of the tent, louder and louder.

An awful racket jolted Mac and Andrew out of sleep. They jumped to their feet. Mac went for the door, but Andrew snagged his arm. "Stop!" he whispered. "It might be a bear."

Mac felt his heart thump. "Bear?" He took a peek. Relief sheeted over him. "It's a raccoon. It's trying to get into the garbage can, but the lid is on too tight."

"From now on, we have to store the trash and food a lot better or this earsplitting racket will keep us up every night," Andrew said, shooing away the raccoon.

"Might be better just to leave leftovers out of the trashcan," Mac said.

Andrew snorted. "Yeah, right. Then the bears smell it and we really have a problem on our hands. Let's just set the trashcan adrift in the pond for tonight."

"Raccoons can swim, Uncle Andrew."

Andrew jammed his hands into his hips. "You going to climb one of these trees at this hour just to hang garbage?"

Mac spun toward the tent. "Hope that raccoon hates water."

Mac and Andrew managed to get some shut-eye, then after breakfast, Mac phoned us. "We're packing up and setting out toward Mount MacKensie," Mac said.

Brad chuckled. "Nice name."

Leaving Small Pond far behind, they entered an extensive plain. Andrew dismounted then bent at the knees and inspected the ground. "All this grass makes for excellent grazing."

Mac shielded his eyes and scanned the horizon. "This plain goes on forever. Wonder how much Frank owns?"

Andrew stood up, slapping his hands together. "I see rooftops west of here. Let's head there." He hurled himself into the saddle then poked his heels into Sarge.

"Watch out for the critter holes, Uncle Andrew. We don't want the horses stepping in one and breaking a leg."

"Take a look at the jackrabbit coming out of that sage," Andrew said, pointing. "Bet you nine-to-one its burrow is under there."

"Over there, Uncle Andrew!" Mac was now pointing. "Another rabbit! Look at it! It's huge!"

"The other one's mate," Andrew said.

Mac's cell phone rang. "Yeah! Hi, Brad! Uh-huh, got a good strong signal. No, I haven't had to plug in the spare battery yet. Now? We're crossing a big grassy plain. Jackrabbits galore! Lots of potholes. Say, does Frank own any of this? Let me know, okay? We're headed west. Looks to be a town. I can't believe we didn't think of taking a map. Look at yours and get back to me."

Moments later, Brad called back. "The town is Wilson. As for the plain, Franks believes a quarter of it is a part of our farm."

It took the rest of the day to get even close to Wilson. Mac and Andrew ended up camping for the night beside a narrow brook.

CHAPTER THIRTY-EIGHT

Mac and Andrew rose at first light and after breakfast, set out for Wilson. To the folks thereabouts, the visitors were a sight to see, riding in with a wagonload of gear. Townsfolk stopped to stare with disbelieving eyes.

"Gee, Uncle Andrew, maybe we shouldn't have come here."

"I agree," Andrew said. "I'll backtrack with the horses and call Frank."

"I'm sure everything is okay," Brad said. "I'll go ahead and find out where the town hall is. We need to find out who owns the rest of that plain."

Andrew returned to the brook then checked in with us. I said, "I'll call John and ask if the town is on the up-and-up. Brad's on-line as we speak, looking up Wilson."

"Tell Brad to call Mac on his cell phone," Andrew said. "Odds are he's already tracked down the owner of that land."

Mac was in the diner, talking to folks who had seen him and Andrew ride into town. All were full of questions; and so was Mac. His cell phone rang. "Yeah. I'm okay, Brad. I'm in the town diner. The mayor is John Hope? Thanks for the info. I'll get back to you."

An elderly lady seated at the counter beside Brad pointed her weathered finger at a table in front of the window. "John Hope is over there," she said in a creaky voice. "Mayor always eats his breakfast right there, this time every morning - all by hisself."

John Hope was wiping his mouth with a napkin. He got to his feet. He was an extremely tall and muscular man with curly black hair. But Mac wasn't intimidated as he slid off the barstool and stepped over to the mayor. "Can I ask you a few questions, sir?"

"Be happy to, son, if you don't mind walking with me a piece."

"Don't mind at all," Mac said.

"Glad to have the company," Hope said. "Do you care to have breakfast? I recommend the blueberry pancakes served by Rose, the finest waitress you'll find anywheres."

"I had breakfast, Mayor, but count on my uncle and me being here first thing tomorrow."

"Call me John. Mr. Hope is my Dad."

"I'm Mac Burns. My partner, Brad Brendan, and I are putting together a cattle ranch to add to a dairy farm owned by his father, Frank Brendan. Frank owns a large forest beyond their barns and part of the plain east of here. My Uncle Andrew and I are here to find out who owns that plain, so we can buy it and graze cattle."

"Yeah, I know who owns it," John Hope said. "Bad news is: The rich son-of-a-gun who owns it intends to save white tail jack rabbits from extinction. He's set in his ways, so don't expect him to sell one square inch of that plain."

"I need to give it a try," Mac said.

The mayor sighed. "Name's Howard Dailey. His place is out of town off Route 142. You'll know it right off the bat. Looks like King Arthur's castle."

Mac frowned. "I better call him first."

The mayor shrugged. "That makes it all the easier for the son-of-a-gun to say no."

The elderly lady, who had been sitting beside Mac, came up and shook her weathered finger. "You're wasting your time, sonny. Dailey don't need a dime and a sharp stick ain't gonna budge him neither."

CHAPTER THIRTY-NINE

Mac called Brad about the conversation with Mayor Hope. In the end they decided the campers should return to Middle. Contact with Howard Dailey was going to be done by car.

"This beats camping out," Andrew said, wolfing down Dolly's apple pie.

"I second that," Mac said, holding out his cup for more coffee.

"Ah-hah!" Dolly exclaimed. "So you do like my coffee!"

"Hey, guys, down to business," Brad said. "I have some ideas about how to approach Howard Dailey. I'm embarrassed say: I'm willing to tell him I'm an injured veteran. He might take pity on me and fulfill my wishes of cattle ranching."

"But he's trying to save jack rabbits from extinction," Mary said.

"I understand that," Brad said, "and it's important he knows we understand. I looked up jack rabbits on line and his concern is valid. Still, I think grazing cattle on that plain doesn't pose a threat to those rabbits."

"However, our horses might break their legs stepping into those holes," I said.

"After being out there," Mac said, "I'm willing to take that chance."

"Then it's settled," Brad said. "We take the van and pay Mr. Daily a visit. That high mucky-muck is going to meet this injured veteran in person."

I watched as Brad and Sky settled into the back of the van and Mac climbed into the driver's seat. Mary rode in front passenger seat. Later, Brad told me, about events that occurred after the van turned onto Route 142:

John Hope was right about knowing Howard Dailey's home "right off the bat." The place *shouted* wealth. "No way are we ever going to convince this guy to give up that plain." Brad said to fellow passengers.

"We're not giving up," Sky said, squinting at the massive gate that blocked the long driveway, which ended at the castle.

A voice erupted from the speakers, which were embedded in the brick gateposts, "May I help you?"

"I am Mac Burns. My friends and I are here to speak with Mr. Dailey regarding the extinction of the white tail jack rabbit."

Five minutes passed. "I don't think he's going to let us in," Mary whispered. "Maybe we should leave and..."

A man came marching down the driveway. His build screamed: Bouncer! He opened the gate then stepped to the driver's window. "I'm Rusty Gannon. The gate isn't working right, so I came to open it. Mr. Dailey is out back, enjoying this gorgeous day. He asked me to direct you to him. He appreciates people stopping by to talk about jack rabbits. If you let me brace myself on your rear bumper and hold onto the roof rack, you can drive up to the house."

"Sure thing," Mac said.

As Rusty attached himself to the back of the van, Sky whispered, "Well Brad, I hope you can carry on a good conversation about jack rabbits."

After they parked, Rusty watched Brad get out of the back of the van. He didn't ask about Brad's injuries. It seemed he already knew the answers: Been there; done that. "I'll get the butler to bring lemonade and chocolate chip cookies."

Brad steered the wheelchair around the house. Mac, Mary, and Sky followed. In the back yard, a small, gray, rickety man was sitting near a dock that extended out into a dazzling lake. The lush green of the gently rolling hills obscured the lake from the front of the house. An array of colorful chairs and bistro tables invited relaxation.

Howard Dailey spoke slowly, using few words, clearly, and without effort. "Come. Sit down. Please."

Mac offered his hand to Dailey. "I'm Mac. This is my wife-to-be, Mary, and this is my friend, Brad, and his wife, Sky."

No sooner had the visitors sat down when Rusty appeared with the butler who was carrying a silver tray loaded the promised goodies. The butler placed the tray on a serving table then poured glasses of lemonade. He gave a glass to each person then offered chocolate chip cookies. Sky took one, saying, "This is a lovely spot, Mr. Dailey. What's the name of this lake?"

"Lake View, which prompted the name of the town, Lakeview, the center of which lies on the opposite shore. Lake View boasts a depth of fifty-one feet. No motorboats allowed. It took numerous laws and efforts to clear the water of gasoline, oil, and debris. I used to take that sailboat you see at the end of the dock to dinner in town. I still go, but Rusty captains it now. He tells me you share my interest in white tail jack rabbits."

Brad spoke up, "I learned a lot about them on-line." His knowledge about rabbits surprised everyone. "Sad to think they are endangered."

After nearly an hour, Howard Dailey said, "How is it that a young man such as yourself is confined to a wheelchair?"

Another hour passed as Brad explained his war injuries and Mac revealed his prosthetic leg. He explained how he met Mac. "Bottom line is we have some pretty big plans to start a cattle ranch."

Howard Dailey sighed. "I sensed the jack rabbits were not what brought you here."

Brad continued, "We named our ranch, the Sky Mac Brad Ranch. Mac and his uncle took a camping trip past the woods behind my father's dairy farm. First, you need to know that Uncle Andrew owns a cattle ranch up in Montana and he came here to help us make plans. My father is willing to give us the forest and pond, but when Mac and his uncle saw the plain beyond there, we thought it would be an excellent place for grazing cattle. Frank owns part of the plain, but we wanted to buy the rest, so Mac tracked you down in the town of Wilson. To make a long story short, we're here to ask you to please sell the plain to us."

"I'm sorry." Howard Dailey said. "I have to burst your dream bubble. I am not willing to break my dream bubble, which is to save white tail jack rabbits. I absolutely will not destroy their habitat on that plain. Goodbye to all of you. I wish you well in fulfilling your dream. Rusty, escort these people back to their vehicle."

They were stunned when Howard Daily closed the door on their dreams so quickly. They were so down they couldn't even speak during the drive home. Upon learning of their disappointment, Dolly and I felt as bad as they did. All of us moped about, wondering what to do next.

Leo called and I told him the bad news. "The old geezer won't even rent it to them?" Leo asked.

I hollered over my shoulder, "Hey Brad! Did you ask about renting that plain?"

"I never got a chance, Dad."

I told Leo and he said, "Tell them not to give up. John and I happen to know Howard Dailey very well. We'll drive out there and speak to him on the kids' behalf. I'll get back to you."

As it turned out, Howard Dailey was pleased to have company, even more so, because that company turned out to be his good friends, Leo and John Brendan.

"You mean to tell me Brad and Sky were Brendans?" Dailey asked. "Your nephew and his wife? Come to think of it, I never did hear any last names. Never once did I consider them related to you. So now, I am terribly sorry for turning them down, especially because your nephew and his friend were injured fighting for our country. I must say, though, saving those rabbits remains dear to my heart."

"Of course," John said. "But can't you both have what you both want?"

"What do you mean?"

"Well, cattle don't endanger jack rabbits," John said.

Leo cut in, "In fact, cattle may very well go a long way towards saving those rabbits. Cow pies are good for growing grass - rabbit food."

"See that?" John said. "You can have your cake and eat it, too. Rent the plain to them. Give the war heroes a break and grant their wish."

Howard frowned while pondering the situation. Finally, he smiled. "Go ahead and call your nephew. Invite him, all of them, and of course, you two, to come tomorrow morning at eleven. I'll have my lawyer draw up papers."

"I'll get Lisa to come with us," John said.

"Now wait one gosh-darn moment," Howard spouted. "Lisa Brendan is *my* lawyer!"

CHAPTER FORTY

Mary wanted her mother and grandmother to do the wedding in the old fashioned manner and on a budget. No way were they going to run up their charge cards. On the other hand, Mac's parents wanted a gala affair for their only offspring and had scads of money to pay for it. So the two families compromised: her family did the planning; his family paid the bills. So full steam ahead. The wedding went off without a hitch.

While Mac and Mary honeymooned, Andrew and Bess flew home to give their ranch overdue attention. From now on, emails were to answer the new ranchers' questions.

Brad and Sky continued to work the business. In addition, Brad exercised, getting in shape to be the best cowboy ever. Buddy provided inspiration by sleeping upside down, spread-eagled.

Just about every day, Sky and I rode out to inspect the Sky Mac Brad Ranch. Her mind was constantly making plans for a home nestled against the forest and overlooking Small Pond.

Cabins were built in a number of places to provide shelter for the hands or to stockpile food and supplies. Outhouses were also built.

One day, Brad got an email from Uncle Andrew: The Oklahoma Farm Bureau is having cattle sales, April 19-21. It is touted as a herd builder and accepts all breeds for sale, which includes heifers and bulls. It will be held the Oklahoma City State Fair Grounds. Great time to buy a registered bull and registered heifers. If you want to go, I'll go with you and help pick out good ones. Big bucks for sure, but Bess and I were waiting to use this sale as a wedding gift to Mac and Mary. We also have been rearing a young bull for your ranch. It has great genes.

Brad emailed: Yes! Sky and I want to go! You two spoil all of us. I have been going on-line and I know how valuable a good bull is. How in the world can we say a proper thank you?

Andrew emailed: Bess and I are pleased to do this. Maybe in the future, you kids will do the same thing for someone else just starting out.

Epilogue

This story revealed how I, Frank Brendan, a single man, became a father - twice!

I introduced you to many wonderful folks; none extra special; none any different from folks of other small towns. However, the folks of Middle, Oklahoma - and a dog named Buddy - certainly helped my family and me to fulfill my sky high wishes.

CPSIA information can be obtained at www.ICGtesting.com
Printed in the USA
BVOW010300091112

305122BV00003B/5/P